Juice
Before
Breakfast

HUGO
UYTTENHOVE

& The Thursday Afternoon Sleuths

Other books by Hugo Uyttenhove:

Grand Scale Larceny: The Heist of the Flemish Primitives (2010)
Rembrandt Redux [A Tom Arden Book] (2011)
The Da Vinci Cloth [A Tom Arden Book] (2018)
Mud Cake For Breakfast [A Carolina Arbors Murder Mystery Book] (2019)
No Tacos For Lunch [A Carolina Arbors Murder Mystery Book] (2019)
Little Ace And his Big Adventures [Children's Book] (2020)
Sloppy Joe For Dinner [A Carolina Arbors Murder Mystery Book] (2020)

© 2022 Hugo Uyttenhove
ISBN: 9798351144467
First Edition – September 2022

Notes

This book is the fourth collaboration between Thursday Afternoon Sleuths Book Club members at Carolina Arbors, a Del Webb Community in Durham, North Carolina. Having read thousands of murder mystery books combined, members undertook another effort to contribute to another book in The Carolina Arbors Murder Mystery series. Again, the story takes place in their community and provides the authenticity of their environment in which they introduce characters who may or may not be witnesses to the crime at hand. Story development and sewing all the parts together are the tasks of the principal author. It's up to Detective T.A. Vinder to solve the case, assisted by newly minted detective Ramón Acosta of the Durham Police Department. As usual, the amateur sleuths of the Thursday Afternoon Sleuths Book Club participate in resolving any unanswered questions.

The subject for this murder mystery book was chosen because of the general concern in many retirement communities about the (mis)use of opioids. The reader is encouraged to have an open mind to the statements of the professionals who appear as characters in this book, to wit, Barbara and Dr. Gupta. Consult your medical provider(s) for more answers to legal and illegal drug concerns.

This book is dedicated to Kristin Conrad, my wife and editor for many years, whom I will miss forever. The author wishes to thank the Thursday Afternoon Sleuths authors who have contributed to the book and helped shape the story. A special thanks to Kim Conrad, a harm reduction specialist, for her professional and insightful contribution.

CHARACTERS

BY

SLEUTH CLUB AUTHORS/CHAPTERS

(IN ORDER OF APPEARANCE)

Barbara Niles
by Leslie Abel - Chapters 1 & 36

Susan Hillendale
by Loretta Gibson and Jane Robbins - Chapters 7, 10 & 31

Mary Valero
by Debbie Turner and BonnieWisler - Chapters 14, 17 & 27

Sam Vanderlaan
by Norman Goldstein - Chapters 21, 38 & 41

Charlotte Beaumont
by Carol Cutler - Chapter 24

George Bender
by Hollins Williams - Chapters 28 & 31

Joan Spencer
by Nancy Ratan - Chapter 29

Patrick Conelly
story by Hugo Uyttenhove
Revisions by Sharlene Dunn and Betsy Mead - Chapters 47, 48 & 49

Three Months Ago

Chapter 1

Opioids

Barbara Nyles smiled at the girl behind the counter of the Dunkin' Donuts and said, "Thank you, and stay warm!" as she took her French cruller and coffee with stiff, reddened hands. *Ugh*, she thought. *I hate cool temperatures and strong wind. It's hard on these old arthritic bones.* She hummed along to "Sugar, Sugar" by the Archies, found a seat facing the door, and slipped into the hard, orange plastic chair. *At least the tables aren't sticky,* she thought.

Barbara was very curious why Joan Spencer wanted to meet at the Dunkin' eight miles away when there's a brand-new store so close to Carolina Arbors. Unsurprisingly, several people had called or emailed after her pandemic-forced Zoom presentation on Harm Reduction for the Community Outreach club. She didn't know how many people attended, but she received numerous calls and emails from those who listened. Most wanted to tell her about their friend's or relative's experience with drug addiction and thank her for her time. Some wanted more information on finding affordable treatment options or harm reduction services in the community; a few were nasty. Blaming the person with the addiction and calling her a *Libtard*, or worse. They didn't bother her much. She filed their names away for future reference and prayed that they never needed treatment or interventions.

Joan was different. She was quietly circumspect about her reasons for wanting to meet and a bit dodgy to boot. Curious, Barbara agreed to the meeting. She took a sip of coffee, but it was still way too hot, so she set it, lid off, on the table to cool and took a bite of the donut. At that moment, another woman entered the shop. She seemed about the right age to live in a 55+ community, so Barbara called out to her. "Joan? Is that you?" When she nodded, Barbara told her to grab a coffee and come over.

Soon, Joan joined her at the laminated table but didn't sit. "Could we move over there? This spot is a little cold," she asked. Barbara agreed, and they made their way to a booth in the sun. Joan quickly moved to the seat facing the door, plopped down, and set her massive cinnamon roll and coffee on the table. "Be careful of the coffee. It's really steaming hot. I almost burned my tongue," Barbara told her. Joan nervously glanced around and started twisting her wedding ring. She didn't seem to know where to begin, so Barbara spoke first.

"It's lovely to meet you, Joan. I moved to The Arbors just a few months before Covid hit, so I haven't met many other people besides my immediate neighbors. Let me tell you a little about myself and what I do, uh, I mean did," she said. She remembered Joan's general phone questions and knew what to say.

"Let's see. I was a nurse at a pain clinic on the outskirts of DC in the nineties during the heyday of Oxycontin use. We really thought it was a miracle drug. People that had suffered chronic pain for years, plus folks dying from cancer and people recovering from trauma, got so much relief. We were told that it was almost impossible to become addicted to Oxy. We could up the dosages almost indiscriminately if people had 'breakthrough' pain." She paused for a few more sips.

Joan seemed a bit lost. There were no questions, just a lot of nodding and drinking coffee. Barbara took a sip and focused on Joan.

"Eventually, it became clear to me that Oxy was indeed addictive. I saw my neighbors, people in my church, and solid families torn apart by family members' addiction. When my cousin, a math teacher, for goodness sake, was arrested for heroin possession after being treated for pain following a car accident, I realized I could no longer be part of the pain clinic's program. My undergraduate studies were biology and social work, so I started looking for programs to help people recover from addictions. I was less than impressed by the rehab programs. The recidivism rate was high. Then I heard about Harm Reduction." Barbara paused. Joan was still quiet, and it bothered Barbara. She figured a question would make this a conversation.

"I'm assuming you heard my talk about that, right?"

"Uh-huh," Joan said and took a bite out of her cinnamon roll.

Barbara continued: "I loved working in that arena. When rehab doesn't work, or when folks are resistant to the idea, at least providing clean needles to prevent disease, providing naloxone to treat overdoses, a safe space to take drugs, and alternatives like suboxone along with support groups and therapy to reduce harm, thereby stabilizing a client's life." She paused again. "Sorry to bother you with all of these medical names, but I wanted to tell you that there are options. Anyway, that's my story in a nutshell. So, would you like to tell me a little about you and why you wanted to talk?"

Joan looked straight into her eyes and simply said, "I feel so stupid."

"Are you struggling with drug use?" Barbara asked softly, her Irish gray eyes filled with compassion.

"No, no. Nothing like that," Joan answered quietly, intently staring at the coffee cup.

"Then...?"

"Like many of us, I'm a child of the sixties. Peace, love. Turn on, tune in, drop out. Vietnam protests. The whole nine yards. I did my share of drugs back then. Pot, LSD, 'shrooms. Nothing more. Then I met my husband. We fell in love, married, had babies and lived an average life. We didn't make much money but worked hard and raised great kids."

This time it was Barbara's turn to nod and remain quiet, listening for anything she could pick up on why Joan wanted this meeting.

Joan continued, "I never thought of drugs as particularly dangerous, but I'm starting to wonder after your talk. Can I ask you some questions about addiction?"

Barbara smiled and nodded, and Joan started firing questions at her while constantly checking the parking lot. Who becomes addicted? How does it start? Why doesn't rehab work better? What drugs are common now? Where do they come from? Are the addicts mentally ill? Is drug abuse limited to the poor and criminals? How does Harm Reduction work? And finally, a question that seemed oddly specific. How has Fentanyl become so widespread? *Finally*, Barbara thought.

The discussion lasted for over an hour. Barbara did her best to dispel myths and provide peer-reviewed evidentiary answers. Suddenly, Joan looked at her watch. Her eyes filled with panic. She stood and exclaimed, "I stayed way too long. Thanks for your time, and you were very informative." With that, she grabbed her coat and fairly sprinted for the door.

Barbara sat for a moment longer and realized she still had no idea why they had a clandestine meeting for such general information. *Poor thing,* she thought; *I hope she calls again. So sad. Maybe even traumatized.* With that thought, she bussed the table, grabbed her coat, and headed home.

Chapter 2

Joan Spencer

A persistent morning fog enveloped the sleepy community known as Carolina Arbors like a damp blanket. Checking that the garage door closed correctly, Joan Spencer settled into the Chevy Equinox SUV passenger seat, ready for another trip down south and at least six hours on that dreaded I-95. Going to US-70, the long wait at the light was already annoying because they were the only ones at the intersection this early. Later there would be hundreds of cars, and then the light signal times made sense. So much has changed in the last few years in this area. There were many more new housing developments and apartments, and everyone was always rushing. Her husband was tapping his fingers on the steering wheel, and she was sure he was about to say something when the light turned green. Soon enough, they drove on I-40 toward I-95 and their trek on the busy interstate toward Jacksonville.

How many times had they made this trip? She couldn't remember. She thought they were probably too many at their age, but they were in a rut, and there was no way out. It was this fact that she found challenging to discuss with her husband. She opened a book she'd signed out at an Ocala library two months ago but quickly decided it was still too dark to read. She'd wait until the sun was up and closed her eyes. Driving on the interstate seemed like they were burrowing through an opaque moisture sheet in a white and grey tunnel. The windshield wipers were going at a good clip. Fabio kept to himself. He was a man of few words and always paid good attention to traffic. All he really needed was a cup of coffee, and he had already taken several sips. She drank a bit from the latte she'd made about an hour earlier. She needed a bite. A new sleeve of crackers was on top of her oversized purse. She stuck the round stack in front of her husband, but he shook his head. No words were spoken.

As they took the ramp to I-95 at Benson, the fog appeared dense, and the tunnel effect was broader and more pronounced. So, how many times had they taken this nine-hour drive? Let's see, she figured and calculated counting on her fingers. They moved to Raleigh, North Carolina, in 1996. They rented the house because they didn't know how long they'd stay. When Carolina Arbors opened in 2013, they could rent a place someone had bought as an investment. It was closer to their son, Jason, and the atmosphere of a 55+ community suited them better. They were not alone. Many in the retirement neighborhood had moved there for the sole purpose of being closer to their grandchildren. Jason had moved to Durham when he took up a position at a start-up near the Research Triangle Park. Unfortunately, it became clear that he and Erin, his wife, needed help after a while, as his benefits were not what they'd been before when living in Florida.

Fabio turned on the radio. So much for counting as Joan became distracted. She hated the news as much as choosing sides in the political spectrum. She'd been a bit of an activist at a young age while in college in upstate New York. That was then, and a hell of a lot of things had happened in her life. Of course, she met Fabio and married him less than a year later. They moved quite a lot, bringing up two children, a boy and a girl, and she'd been a full-time homemaker. A yearly vacation of about a week is all they could afford early on. She never joined or belonged to any clubs until Fabio retired. That's when they moved to Florida, just about ten years ago. She was still amazed how they could own one home and rent another one. She smiled when she thought of their community in North Carolina, referred to as an active adult one. Not for her. They kept to themselves, rented, and traveled back and forth to their home in Florida, where they lived in an even bigger adult community. It wasn't easy to keep to themselves. Their neighbors were friendly and kept trying to get to know them and involve them in activities. Fabio had deemed it not necessary.

The news on the radio had quickly become background noise, and she tried to figure it out again. So, in 2016, they went back from November till February the following year. The trouble started after returning to Florida for about four weeks in May, almost three years ago. They went back the same week. Two months later, they drove back down, even though it was hot as hell that spring, only to be needed back in Durham in mid-August.

Bored with whatever he was listening to, Fabio switched the station to sixties music. Anyway, that was two round trips. She couldn't remember whether they returned in October or November. One thing was for sure; it became necessary to make the trip more regularly as the trouble carried on. So, beginning the following year, they went down six times a year and continued even during the pandemic. Quarantining wasn't on their agenda; there were many other things to worry about. Joan was satisfied that she had counted about twenty-plus trips. How many miles was that? Oh, who cared! The important thing was that they could do it and had safely done it as the trouble was being handled and things became more manageable.

Of course, Fabio had wanted to quit this going back and forth. Then again, it appeared it wasn't their choice after all. They did agree that eventually, they'd sell the place in Florida and buy the rental at the Arbors before, as he predicted, the prices would skyrocket. It was not to be, so she'd finally called their constant travel a rut. When would it end?

Chapter 3

Fabio Spencer

Damned fog! Fabio had looked at the weather forecast the evening before. Foggy conditions never got a mention. The white haze bothered him, and Fabio felt he was getting tunnel vision. Luckily for him, coffee and the radio did the trick, allowing him to pay attention to the road. He concluded that he'd become a much better driver in the past few years and took a sip of his favorite dark roast brew. He never went more than four miles over the speed limit. He used his blinkers profusely and kept the car perfectly in its lane. He loved his Chevy. He was told that the vehicle should always be checked for proper lights to avoid being stopped by a trooper. The North Carolina registration, however, was the biggest headache. Going back and forth caused a close call in getting the sticker in time. Between having the vehicle inspected and the check mailed in, there was no telling when the new sticker would arrive. He never bothered with registering the car in Florida. It would have been simpler, but there was no reason to change now, keeping their current plans in mind. Also, they never forwarded their mail, and there was no telling whether a trip might be delayed, which was a problem.

Once on I-40, he'd settled in, hoping for a clearing before they started the leg to the Florida border. Seeing this wasn't the case, he listened to American News on a Sirius XM channel. He didn't care much what they chattered about because they were talking heads who filled up the airwaves with constant comments about whatever ailed the country. Once in a while, he'd pick up something that piqued his interest, but it quickly faded away as he soon lost interest. He was somewhat intrigued by politics but not by people telling him what to think about it. For now, he didn't mind the noise. It seemed better than having to listen to a neighbor who went off on some political issue that needed attention immediately, lest it would cause the end of the world as we knew it. Idiots, he thought. He had better things to do.

They didn't associate much with others and certainly didn't belong to any clubs. When he played golf, he'd show up on a course preferably about an hour away, avoiding having to play with neighbors. Too many nosy ones. Sure, he'd told some that he was a retired construction consultant, but he never went into detail. People always wanted to find out where they were from and when in Florida, he'd say North Carolina. He simply switched the locations when in the other community. It'd been like that for years, and he was okay with it. When someone was more persistent, like a question about where he had grown up, he'd give the proverbial answer as upstate New York. That got a reaction like 'how about them Bills' or, 'I worked in Syracuse.' Upstate had different connotations in the City, so he'd corrected himself several times, divulging he grew up in the Hudson Valley area. This was true, but he never offered more than that and often changed the subject.

He looked at the speedometer and figured that they were making good progress despite the weather conditions. He changed the station to an oldies one and took another sip. He glanced at Joan and saw that she was reading her novel. Earlier in the week, she'd told him it was due soon at the library and that she wanted to finish it before they got home. That's all she did anyway, he reflected. Read and read, the whole trip long. Not much was said, and they seldom talked about their predicament, the family, or the day's events. They had plenty to discuss once at home, but he needed to pay attention to all that was happening around him on the road. Speed traps bothered him, and he usually panicked when an Amber alert increased the possibility of police being on the road. I-95 appeared to be a favorite corridor to take off with a child, and he didn't like that to happen when driving on that road.

Fabio noticed his wife counting something on her fingers. What was she up to? He was tempted to ask, but she soon returned to her book, and he let it slide. Another fifteen minutes and they'd stop for their first meal of the day. Nearing the South Carolina border, the mist finally cleared, and traffic picked up a bit more. They'd be stopping soon for about a good half hour at their favorite spot, where they'd have the usual breakfast and refill their coffee containers. Joan loved the freshly baked biscuits as long as she could enrich them with a firm blob of butter.

All the songs playing on the station were very familiar to him, but he never hummed along. That was too distracting, and he liked it more as background noise. He thought again about their neighbors, especially that woman, Mary Valero, who lived next door at the Arbors. He was sure she'd given up inviting them over for a drink, barbecue, or whatever. They'd turned those offers down so many times. Socializing was a risk rooted in his fear that something might slip and cause suspicion. Of course, he'd seen the disappointment on Mary's face. Even though she'd stopped asking, she remained very friendly, always said hello and knew when an already short conversation had to end. In that respect, Fabio felt he had trained the neighbors well. The neighbor on the other side, Joe Malinski, was a New Yorker, but they'd shied away from him when he turned out to be an ex-detective. Likewise, Fabio felt they'd trained their neighbors in Florida equally well.

He cleared his throat to signal Joan that he was about to get off the highway.

Chapter 4

Cracker Barrel

The Spencers always went to the same restaurant chain. They liked the comfort food and, most of all, the prices. They were patrons even when their children were young. The go-to dinner in those days was mac and cheese, while biscuits easily satisfied hungry stomachs. Nowadays, they'd go for chicken and mashed potatoes. The all-day breakfast menu would serve them well at Cracker Barrel this morning.

Fabio always parked with the car's rear towards a restaurant window that showed open seating. He had argued that keeping an eye on the vehicle while sitting down was essential. Having accomplished this again, they sat by the big window and ordered pancakes, eggs and bacon. The waitress filled their coffee mugs and walked away. Joan started the conversation.

"So, you were quiet this morning. Anything on your mind that you want to share?"

"Not very much. You know very well that I need to keep an eye on the road, even going to Florida, although it's less stressful."

"Relax, Fabio. No one is looking for us."

"I know that, but we're not driving empty this time...."

"What? What are you talking about?"

"Shh! Keep your voice down," Fabio whispered. He looked left and right in the sparsely occupied restaurant. "I didn't want to tell you. Anyway,...."

"Tell me what?"

"Our Durham guy asked me to take a small box and give it to the Ocala guy as soon as possible after we get home."

"And what do you think is in that box?"

"It's not very heavy. Maybe it's cash. Money?"

"That's a new one. What would happen if we got caught with that?"

"Exactly what I'm worried about. We wouldn't be able to explain where it came from or what we'd do with it."

"How much is it, you think?"

"If they're all twenties, I think about 20K, but if they're hundreds, you figure."

"Why didn't you tell me about that before we left?"

"Didn't want to worry you. Anyway, we're making good progress, and we can get rid of it tomorrow."

"I'd feel better if you got rid of it today. I'm going to be nervous till then."

"Okay then. Consider it done. I'll text the guy as soon as we get in," Fabio said as he looked up toward the waitress. "Ah, food. Thanks. I'm starved."

Once they sorted out their plates, both poured too much syrup on the pancakes, and Joan over-buttered her biscuit. She stared out the window at the back of their Chevy and shook her head. Instead of simplifying things soon, it now appeared her husband got them in deeper.

The waitress refilled their mugs, and Fabio poured his coffee straight into his travel cup. "So, I think we'll stop one more time and then should make it back home around 4:30," he continued the conversation.

"Fine. I can do some shopping when you get back because we don't have anything for dinner," Joan said and dug into the eggs and bacon.

"Sounds good."

After a short silence, Joan put her knife and fork down. "Did you get the impression Ellie looked better yesterday?"

"Ellie? Let me think. She didn't look so pale. She may have been excited about something. Honestly, I don't know. She's been through a lot, but her future looks promising. Every day I'm so grateful that we were able to help."

"She was hoping to see us again soon. She told me she wants to go on a long walk."

"Well, that's positive. I'm sure it was all worth it."

"Of course it was," Joan said, picking up her utensils. She rested her fists on the table with the knife and fork sticking up. "No second-guessing here. We made a choice, and it was good." This time, she stressed the word *was*.

"I hear a *but* coming," Fabio sighed.

"Ah, you're so smart and so right. Yes, I think we need to consider an exit strategy here."

It was now Fabio's turn to weaponize his utensils. "Wait, we've already talked about that. It's not that easy. Where does this come from anyway? I don't think we're ready yet."

"How much longer can we do this?"

"I don't know, but I think maybe another six months? I, too, want to sell the place in Florida. That would be the end of it. Anyway, I'll do some calculations when we get home, and we can discuss it then. This is not the place to talk about this."

"Okay, but I'm holding you to this," Joan said, and before continuing her breakfast, she briefly glanced outside. A police car had pulled up on the other side of the parking lot, opposite their SUV. "Hey, look. Cop over there." Joan had become paranoid every time she saw a police car. She couldn't imagine what she'd do if they were stopped for some traffic violation. She was sure she'd get so nervous that any officer would get suspicious.

"Don't panic," Fabio said and smiled halfheartedly. "There's no reason he would check out our car."

"You're right. He's already leaving."

"See, no problem," Fabio grinned.

Ten minutes later, they were on the road again. Joan continued reading her book while Fabio was listening to his oldies. He checked the time and spoke the only words for quite a while. "We should be home on time."

Chapter 5

Home Again

As predicted, at 4:30 PM, the Spencers pulled onto Buena Vista Boulevard and, minutes later, via Bailey Trail and the sidestreet they lived on, parked in the driveway of their small ranch-style home. Even though it was May, the humidity was palpable, and it felt like 90 degrees. The lawn appeared mowed and trimmed, and everything looked okay at first glance. After all, Joan said, we were gone for six weeks, and with all the storms they'd heard about, one never knows. Then again, their neighbor, Susan, would've called if something was amiss.

Fabio walked inside via the front door, went into the garage via the kitchen and plugged in the garage door opener. They never left the power on in the garage while gone. He believed too many people had garage door openers that worked for someone else's garage. Since they didn't have an alarm, good keys and no electronics to open the garage, the front door was the safest, Fabio figured. He advanced the Equinox into its spot next to the water heater. He also turned on that unit.

Inside, it was about 76 degrees, and they could afford to set the thermostat a few degrees lower now that they were home again. Joan had already taken her suitcase to the bedroom, and Fabio brought in his. He had left a large cardboard box in the living room. He returned to it and opened it, and lifted a plastic-wrapped package from it. Looking around, he decided to put it on top of a cabinet.

He sat down and looked up a contact on his phone. It wasn't even a name but rather a short number to which he could send a text. The corresponding number was only valid for a week, sometimes for only a few days. Sure enough, after messaging Back at the ranch, the agreed to code, the message kicked back. Damn! He had been afraid of that. The number was no longer in use. Fabio took a deep breath. Yes, perhaps a new number was left on their landline's voicemail.

The first fifteen messages were about car warranty expiration and insurance options. Judging by its content, he listened to a personal message intended for him and his wife. At first, he wasn't sure it meant anything, almost causing him to erase it. On second thought, he listened again: *"Hey, it's me again. Change in plans. Stop by in Durham for a present. I will text you on Monday."*

Fabio couldn't figure it out. Today was Tuesday, and he didn't recall getting a text from anyone. Then, he noticed that the message was dated over three weeks ago. He listened to the rest of the voice messages, deleting them all. He hurried to the bedroom, where his wife hung clothes in their closet.

"I just listened to the strangest message."

"Oh, from someone we know?" Joan asked.

"Doubt it. It was sent three weeks ago. I don't recognize the voice at all."

"What was it about then?"

"About picking up a present in Durham. It doesn't make sense. We only pick up presents in Ocala. Also, when the message was left three weeks ago, we were in Durham. It's gotta be a mistake or wrong number."

"I don't think so," Joan said and turned around, holding an empty hanger. "Stopping by for a present is the usual phrase, isn't it?"

"I realize that, but we never pick anything up in Durham."

"You did pick up the money, right?"

"That was called a gift by our man there."

"Present or gift, what difference does it make?"

"None, I guess, but I never got a text as the caller said I would."

"Well, I really want to know when you'll get rid of that money."

"That's a funny thing too. I tried to send a message to the number we were given, and it was rejected."

"Oh. Now, that's no good. If you don't deliver that quickly, who knows, people will come looking for it, and I don't like that one bit."

"I know all that. I just don't have anyone to call."

"Text the guy in Durham."

"I guess I could do that."

"Meanwhile, what have you done with the money?"

"I put it on top of the tall cabinet. It's out of sight."

"Good. Let me know what the guy in Durham says."

Fabio returned to the living room and texted his Durham contact: **Gift arrived OK in FL – who gets it?**

It took less than ten seconds for the response: **Will text address. Had issues. Take it there tomorrow 9 PM.**

Fabio waited for the follow-up message and figured he'd send another message: **Was I supposed to pick up a present in Durham?**

Again, the answer was almost immediate: **No, I gave you a gift – not a present – wtf?**

He couldn't explain it and simply answered: **There was a message on my phone to pick it up in Durham. It was three weeks ago.**

It took about five minutes for an answer to appear: **Do you have a number of the voice mail?**

No, it was an unknown number.

It remained silent for a short while. Fabio got up as a new text appeared: **Disregard. If it happens again, text me. Will text a new number in a few minutes. Be on time tomorrow night.**

As there was nothing more to add, Fabio turned off his phone, and his wife walked in. "All set for the money. Taking it to Ocala tomorrow eve."

"Good, the sooner it's out of here, the better. I'm a bit nervous having it here at the house, though."

"It'll be alright."

"Maybe we can talk about the house here in The Villages after dinner?"

"Sure, but remember what I said; it may not be up to us."

Joan kept unpacking as she was thinking about her conversation with Barbara. This business of picking up and delivering boxes had to stop. She decided that she needed to put her foot down.

Chapter 6

Senior Living

Even though they loved living in North Carolina, many small things made their home in The Villages special and perhaps hard to part with now. Joan stood by the citrus trees in the backyard. The three trees really covered all of the backyard. The navel orange tree was doing well, but it already had its fruit in January. On the other hand, the Meyer lemons were very ripe and ready to pick. She planned to pick most of them later in the week and take at least fifty back to Durham. Her favorite tree bearing about forty ruby red grapefruits was near their neighbor Susan's house, where only orange trees grew. Susan always asked for some of the ruby fruit. However, it would be at least six weeks before those would be ripe.

Thinking of Susan, Joan was surprised she hadn't seen her neighbor yet. The woman usually kept an eye out for anything that went on in their street, and for sure, she'd seen them come in yesterday. Susan was a widow who'd lived in Florida for about fifteen years. She and her husband Tom had moved from Buffalo and had retired early. Both were avid golfers, and ever since she was alone, she'd kept up the sport. She owned a nice golf cart and used it to travel everywhere within the community of over 55,000 homes. Golf was something Joan didn't care about much. Even Fabio hadn't played in a while. They got confused or surprised looks when they told neighbors they didn't play. As a matter of fact, there were many things they didn't participate in at the Villages. That hadn't always been the case. They stopped it all when they started their trips to North Carolina. Once they were inconsistently away to their house at the Arbors, there was an apparent reason for not joining any clubs. There was simply no time to commit, and it suited them fine.

Life in the Villages differed significantly from the retirement community's life up north. The day they moved into their new home, they visited a golf cart store and ordered a shiny dark blue cart. It had all the bells and whistles, and its gas engine was relatively quiet. Like so many others, the cart became their primary form of transportation. They often got lost as none of their destinations could be reached in a straight line. They sometimes had to navigate a tunnel or a bridge and take shortcuts through parking lots and small streets in another village. Although they only lived ten minutes by car from the square at Spanish Springs, their first ride there took about an hour. Once they figured it out, Joan even dared to go shopping at the nearest Publix, securing her groceries with a rope in the cart.

Then there was happy hour! Joan and Fabio were not big drinkers, but a free beer or a glass of cheap wine didn't make them stay away. They used to join neighbors around four in the afternoon, and by five-thirty, most panicked about dinner not being ready. They thought it was funny, but they were on a similar schedule less than a year later. All was good; the weather was excellent most of the time, and living was good. Then, years later, when the trouble began, things changed, and their first step was to sell their golf cart. Getting rid of a symbol of their area was almost unheard of then. When neighbors, especially Susan, inquired what was going on, Fabio blamed his age and their frequent travels to Durham as the main reason. Joan started driving with Susan to various places. Still, their neighborly friendship ended when the money from the golf cart was gone. Then one day, they met a nice fellow at a pizza parlor, and the rest of the story manifested itself in their current lifestyle. They were made a one-time offer they couldn't refuse, and their trips up north started regularly. Joan's friendship with Susan waned, and soon they kept to themselves.

Joan stood by the grapefruit tree and saw Susan peeking behind a curtain. Joan was about to wave when the curtain snapped back. Susan didn't come through the back door, so Joan decided to go back in. It was best to remind Fabio of the package he had to deliver.

Chapter 7

Susan

Susan Hillendale noticed that the Spencers were back in the Villages again, returning from North Carolina. It was hard to say how long Joan and Fabio had been away this time. Had it been just a couple of weeks, or was it a month or longer? She thought it strange how they went back and forth between their two homes with no set pattern. Almost everyone at The Villages who had another house came down in the late fall and then retreated to their other place in the spring. But that's not true for the Spencers. To Susan, it was worrisome because it was so random. She also realized that she hadn't seen their daughter or son and his family for over a year. Their granddaughter, Ellie, was such a cute five-year-old when she saw her last. Florida was a good destination for everyone. Most Villages residents invited their relatives to enjoy the amenities and see how much the place offered their Boomer parents.

Thinking more about that, Susan noticed that Joan and Fabio no longer participated in clubs, happy hours, dances, or other social events. What was up with that? She wanted to find out why because it was driving her crazy. But could Joan's aloofness be from something she said or did? It was awkward that Susan knew Joan saw her peeking at her through the window. She knew it was unfriendly, but the Spencers never bothered to notify her when they arrived, so how else was she supposed to know when they came home? Maybe she'll mention it the next time she sees her?

Susan knew that Joan had belonged to many clubs in The Villages. When she looked it up in the community directory, Joan was listed as a member of six clubs. They varied from the Line Dancing Club, the Hiking Club, the Wine Club, and one of the many book clubs. Susan has always thought that Joan was active, social, and fun to be around. She liked to party, dance, and drink, socially, of course. But something had changed over the last years, with her not getting involved in anything anymore. Why was that?

That night, Susan couldn't sleep as she worried about Joan. As a widow without family nearby, Susan sometimes felt alone and wished she had a better relationship with Joan. Tossing around in bed, Susan decided to renew her friendship with Joan and Fabio. Maybe once she got close to Joan again, she would get her to tell her what was happening in her family. As she drifted off to sleep, she wondered whether the Spencers were somehow in trouble. Maybe one of them had a fatal disease and needed to travel to hospitals near their home in North Carolina? Who knew, but perhaps the Mafia was after them for some reason, or maybe they owed money and ran from creditors? Well, she would have to wait until another day to find out.

The following morning, Susan walked over to the Spencers to welcome them back with fresh coffee and donuts.

When the door opened and Fabio appeared, she smiled graciously and said, "Welcome back! Hope traffic on I-95 wasn't too bad."

"Same as usual," Fabio responded somewhat nonchalantly as Joan joined him at the doorstep.

"So, you're back so soon this time. Is everything okay?"

"Oh, we're just fine. We wanted a bit of sunshine." Joan chimed in.

"Is your son coming to visit sometime?"

"No, he's swamped, working at his start-up company."

"Are you going to buy another golf cart? I'm happy to take you some places, but it's convenient to have your own golf cart."

"No," Joan answered. "No plans to get another cart, but it would be nice to go with you shopping once in a while."

"It's just that I've missed having you around. I thought we could catch up and go to happy hour together sometime," said Susan, disappointed.

"I'll check my schedule and call you," Joan smiled.

"Looking forward to it," Susan said and handed them the coffee and donuts. "Enjoy!"

Fabio took the goodies and said thank you. The door closed.

That afternoon, Susan wondered whether the Spencers figured her too inquisitive. She didn't want to come across as a nosy neighbor, but what else was she supposed to do to keep herself busy? Hopefully, her relationship with Joan was on the mend now. Still, it's Fabio whose personality has really changed over the years, she concluded. Lately, he pretty much kept to himself. He used to be more outgoing and fun-loving and belonged to a few clubs. He shared membership with Joan in some, but his favorites had been the Financial Investment Club and Habitat for Humanity Club. The latter allowed him to join fellow members on long weekend trips when they built homes for disabled Veterans. Nowadays, he doesn't belong to any club. Susan was surprised he even showed up at the door first.

Later in the afternoon, Susan had stepped outside to sweep the walkway from her driveway to her front door and saw Fabio putting his golf clubs in his SUV. She figured that was odd since she was told he had stopped playing golf. Apparently, that must have meant he didn't play golf on one of their many courses. So, where was he playing then, and whom did he play with?

Back inside her home, Susan had the distinct impression that Fabio acted strangely around her. It was as if the less he said, the less likely he'd say something wrong. She shrugged it off, joking that he probably hid a big secret. Regardless of what it was, Susan decided to get to the bottom of it. Nothing else to do, she figured.

Chapter 8

Ocala

The money package was secured inside the large side pocket of his golf bag where he usually put his shoes. Fabio covered the bag with a blanket in the trunk of his car. He had looked at the route and figured out how to get there. He estimated it would take him about forty-five minutes to the drop-off address. Not wanting to be distracted, he turned his GPS off. The last thing he wanted was for the police to stop him for crossing a line or swerving while checking the small screen.

Traffic was light, and it took about the estimated time. The address took him to a deserted strip mall where all the stores were closed. A black sedan was parked near a line of shrubs. A man inside flashed the lights, and Fabio drove straight to the vehicle. He backed up into the parking spot next to the car, as was their standard method of keeping the trunk away from any cameras or on-lookers whenever he went to a drop point.

Fabio turned off his lights, got out, walked to the back of his car and opened the trunk. The man in the adjoining car likewise opened the trunk of his car. Both men felt safe in being shielded from potential on-lookers. Fabio had never met this contact before. He assumed he was South American, seeing the short and stocky man sporting a thick black mustache and a gruff beard on a darkly tanned face. The man spoke first. "You're a punctual man. I like that."

"I was told here to be by nine."

"Good," the man said. "Where's the package?"

Fabio moved the blanket and unzipped the side pocket of his golf bag. He pried the package out of it. "Here you go."

The man opened the spare tire area in the trunk of his car and tucked the grey package into the back, putting the lid back on the cavity. "From now on, you'll bring a package like that to me. I'll let you know where each time."

"So, every two months then?"

"No, it will be every month from now on."

"What do you mean?"

"The boss wants you to bring it every month. Banks have made it too difficult for us."

"Are you telling me we need to travel back and forth every month?"

"Yes. The boss says you'll be compensated when back in North Carolina. Five grand a month extra money, señior."

"I don't care about the money. That's too much travel for us. My wife won't like it, and I don't either. Tell your boss we've done our share, and he needs to find someone else. I don't think I need to go into detail about our changed situation."

"I don't want to hear about your situation. We all do what the boss says, or..."

"Or what?" Fabio said rather loudly.

"Keep your voice down."

"Or what?" Fabio repeated.

"You don't want to know. You can't quit now. You guys are great. There's no reason to change anything now. The boss doesn't like people quitting on him. He's done bad things to those who have tried."

Fabio closed the back of the SUV. He wanted to sound resolute, but his voice quivered when he spoke. "Regardless. Tell him we're out. We want to sell our place here in Florida. He can't make us take all that stuff up north forever."

"You have no idea of what he can do. I remember a couple like you whose car ran off the road. They didn't make it."

Fabio stood frozen and felt dizzy. This couldn't possibly be the way things were going to be. He took a deep breath and reflected on how he'd need to speak to his regular contact. At least that man understood why and how long they'd be making those trips. The man here, however, was threatening them. He felt his hand shaking and tried to steady his nerves. Obviously, this wasn't what they signed up for, and this man was not the one to argue with. He wanted to get home as soon as possible. "Well, we'll see," he said, walking to the driver's side door. "Tell your boss we plan a final trip to North Carolina."

"Oh, I'll pass it on. All I know is that you're scheduled to go soon. Be ready for a pick-up in a few days. Business is increasing, you see. I hope you get what I mean," the man said as he closed his trunk. "You can make so much money, senor!" He got in his car, and without another word, he drove off, tires screeching as if to put an exclamation point after the last words.

Fabio stood still, watching the red lights disappear on the road. He knew Joan really wanted out, and now it appeared it wasn't their decision. He realized he'd have to have a different conversation with her soon.

Chapter 9

Plans

The following day, Fabio didn't feel like elaborating with Joan on his conversation with the man in the parking lot. When he returned, he only mentioned to his wife that the drop-off went fine. He left it at that, as she seemed caught up in her thoughts or was tired. However, Joan became more inquisitive over coffee while reading The Villages Daily Sun. She needed to know what the future held for them.

"So, had you seen the guy from last night before?"

"Nope. I think he was Hispanic, and his English was pretty good."

"Did he say when our next trip needed to be made?"

"Yes and no," Fabio offered, turning a page and pretending to read something interesting, unable to explain his dual answer.

"So he did give us a date?"

"He said something about giving him another package in about a month. He told me that I may have to pick a package in a few days."

Joan frowned. "No way! We weren't returning to the Arbors until about three weeks. This back and forth within weeks wasn't part of the deal."

"I know that. Our usual guy has not told us anything about this, so I'm taking it with a grain of salt."

"I think you should get in touch with him. It would be good to make these people realize that we're done with this."

"You're talking about an exit strategy again, but I don't think it's ours to make."

"What do you mean? When we quit, that's it! We'll sell this place and buy the house at the Arbors. What's so..."

"Hold on, Joan," Fabio snapped, stopping her mid-sentence. "You're not listening. I told you, it's not our decision."

"Why not? What are you talking about?"

"The fellow last night indicated that it would be the big boss who decides that."

"I don't believe that. After selling this place, we pack things up and make one last trip to North Carolina! It's as simple as that, Fabio. Really."

"They wouldn't let us, I'm afraid."

"Listen, once we are out of here, we're no use to them."

"They don't look at it that way. They count on us," Fabio said, still hesitant in telling her what the Latino man had said.

"They can't make us drive up and down again. That's ridiculous."

Fabio bit his bottom lip. He'd never kept secrets from Joan, but he'd sugar-coated it first whenever there had been bad news. In this instance, he felt he had no choice but to tell her what he understood to be the larger picture. He decided to be blunt and put down the paper. "Listen, honey. It's complicated. Another couple who refused to make the runs any longer had a bad accident on the road."

"No!" Joan yelled as she stood up. Grabbing the coffee pot, she shook her head. "Anyone can have an accident. I'd find it hard to believe if you imply that those men had something to do with that. Why would they do such a thing?"

"That couple, just like us, had become essential to their business."

"So, what happened to the couple after the accident?"

"They didn't make it."

Except for a sudden gasp by Joan, as she put her hand over her mouth, there was immediate silence, and both husband and wife just stared at each other. Something had finally sunk in about being a small cog in a giant wheel of drug transportation. Joan swallowed hard and sat down again. "Okay then. We'll figure this out and won't tell them about selling this house. We'll go up north the last time after we close. They won't know a thing, and we'll make it without incident. You make the last drop, and that's it."

Fabio folded the paper. "Yeah, easily said, dear. They know where we are at the Arbors. These people will find us in no time."

"Then we go away for a while. A vacation. Perfect! Finally!" Joan said sternly.

Fabio shook his head. His wife was often poised to take the lead with headstrong conviction. Indeed she'd seen enough crime stories on TV, he thought. "And how long do you plan on us being gone?"

"Maybe a month or a bit longer."

"Once we return, we'd have the same problem."

"Well, dammit," Joan said. "We have to stop all this."

"I know, but just a few days ago, you didn't seem to mind that we'd continue till the end of the year or so."

"Well, I changed my mind. I've done some reading, and I talked to someone who knew all about illegal drugs. They are horrible, and I'm not kidding. Do you know people can die from taking them? So, here we are, aiding people dying while our single purpose was to prevent someone from dying! This is the worst thing we've ever done, Fabio." Joan grabbed her husband's hands, and tears welled up.

Fabio saw it as a sign that her commitment to their money-making trips was showing severe cracks. "We knew going in that what we did wasn't kosher. At the time, we figured someone needed to do this, and we were told that this was the only way to get what many people needed. We needed the money, and we got lots of it."

"Well, I'm over that. Often people become addicted to those drugs. I couldn't believe it when I heard how many people die of overdoses."

"Not with the stuff we bring over, right?"

"We don't know that. It may be, and the whole opioid thing has become a real problem in North Carolina and the whole country. I read that retirement communities are using these kinds of opioids."

"They just get what their doctor would otherwise prescribe."

"In some cases, maybe, yes. The person I talked with emphasized addiction. There's a reason doctors won't prescribe any more of those meds. People get it differently and sometimes take a bad version of the synthetic opioid. Overdoses happen when people use a substance different from what they think it is. It can be toxic, and that is what causes overdoses. That's the problem."

"I still think there's a legitimate reason for people to get whatever we brought up. We don't see proof that these particular drugs cause addiction or overdosing," Fabio dismissed his wife's last comment.

"I think you should read up on it, dear. We need to stop this. I wouldn't want to have the death of a single person in our community on our conscience."

"Judging by what you said the last few minutes, I think we may have passed that," her husband said, shaking his head as her words sank in. He now experienced that same nauseating feeling he experienced the night before when talking to the man.

Joan shook her head and cleared the dishes from the table. "Still, I want us to quit those runs now. No more taking that stuff."

"As I said, they'll give us another package in a few days, and we have no other choice. We'd have to leave in less than three weeks and return immediately. There's no way we can sell the house before then."

"I think we can. There's a real estate agent just outside The Villages, and I hear she sells homes quickly."

"Everything is recorded, and anyone can see the deeds online. They'd find us in a heartbeat."

"Then what do you suggest?" "Go to the police?" Joan asked, putting the dishes in the sink.

"Of course not. Are you crazy? Honey, they'd make sure we had new accommodations, alright. Jail! So, no way."

It remained quiet for a while as Joan let that one sink in. In the living room, she mindlessly repositioned some knickknacks in no particular way. Fabio knew his wife was letting things settle in her mind. She was right, of course; they'd have to develop some plan, but the current ideas were not the ones that would keep them from harm. Perhaps their regular contact could introduce them to that boss, whoever that was. He walked up behind his wife and softly put his hand on her shoulder. "I know you're upset, honey. But let's think about this for a while. We have time. I'll call our guy if you agree and get through to the boss."

Joan turned around, her eyes red and tears running freely along the lines on her cheek to her mouth. "Oh, Fabio, what have we done?"

Chapter 10

The Square

Susan's curiosity hadn't diminished since her brief morning conversation with the Spencers a few days ago. She really wanted to be friends with them, and as a widow, living alone was getting old. Besides needing companionship, Susan was determined to find out what was going on in the life of her neighbors. She was convinced that the only way to do that was to spend more time with Joan. She thought of all the possibilities that could be interesting for Joan, such as shopping, going out to lunch or other fun things like getting their nails done. The next day, Susan came up with the idea of taking care of her loneliness and getting together with Joan. She was hoping, of course, that she'd get Joan to talk openly.

Joan had answered the door, and Susan was straightforward when telling her neighbor she needed to be her wingman to have some fun on Friday night. She suggested they go to the World of Beer bar and wander over to Spanish Springs

Square, where her favorite band, the Anita Drink Band, would perform live. To her surprise, Joan accepted the invitation.

Susan was in a great mood when she drove her golf cart to her neighbor's driveway a little before 4:30 PM that Friday. They chatted all the way to the square about life in The Villages. Once at Spanish Springs, they got good seats, and Susan got a few drinks from the beer specialty store.

After a few songs, Susan noticed Joan having a great time. The band played, and Joan moved her body rhythmically with the beat as if dancing in her chair. With all the tension of the past few days, Joan seemed to need this outing more than Susan did. They enjoyed the band playing Rock & Roll, Soul, Disco, Funk and Motown tunes. There was more going on than just moving with the music. Susan noticed a few single men sitting on a bench, glancing in their direction. As she figured, a slow tune was playing, and two men approached them and asked to dance. Joan hesitated, but a tall white-haired gentleman took her hand and off she went dancing. *Totally uncharacteristic for her,* Joan thought. While some of the bars in The Villages were known as "shark tanks" for men and women to ogle each other, dance, and even sometimes leave together, the Square was no different.

Susan looked over her shoulder as she danced with another man. It was strange as she'd never danced again since her husband's passing. Susan missed her Tom a lot. But when encouraging Joan to dance, she felt like she had to do the same. Joan liked to dance, and she appeared pretty chatty with her partner. Susan, however, felt kind of sad thinking about Tom. She needed to focus on her mission, and if Joan drank too much or, God forbid, if she took off with the tall guy, she wouldn't get the answers to her questions. After the second dance, she told Joan they should retake their seats.

The concessions stand at the Square always had a two-for-one special on drinks. Joan bought one of their specialties: Peach Whiskey Sours. The band took a five-minute break and, seeing a relaxed Joan, Susan saw her opportunity to get her to answer some questions she had been dying to ask. "Hey Joan, are you having a good time?"

Joan smiled. "I haven't had a drink in two years, and I haven't danced for years." She put a finger up to her lips and giggled. "But don't tell Fabio!"

"Well, I'm glad we're doing it then," Susan said. She put her hand on Joan's arm and leaned in. "I hope you don't think I'm being nosy or anything. I've wondered why Jason, his wife, and Ellie haven't been down to The Villages in quite a long time. Is everything okay with them? It seems you guys go up there often lately. Is little Ellie okay"

"Oh sure, of course," Joan answered hesitantly. "Jason's startup company in Durham has kept him really busy."

"Are you sure everything is alright?" Susan persisted.

Joan looked away, grinning at a seventy-something man with a fedora approaching the table so she didn't have to answer Susan. The band had started to play again. She'd been nervous and agitated since she talked with Barbara in Durham. Then there was that article in the newspaper yesterday. Before she looked back at Susan, she thought it might be a good idea to talk about it since it bothered her. Then again, maybe she should leave it alone now that she and Fabio were about to make critical decisions. She took a huge swig of her drink, trying to appear calm. Before answering her friend, she considered that perhaps Susan could help, in some way, get them out of this mess. She really liked the music and the ambiance in the square, which reminded her of the fun times she had with her husband years ago. She felt tired of driving back and forth and being careful every minute. Then she changed her mind. There's no way she could tell Susan anything. If they wanted to leave secretly, there was no point in sharing that information. She got up and took the hand of the man with the fedora hat.

Susan could tell that something was up and that Joan was struggling with something. After all, her question hadn't been answered. She took a few more sips while the couple danced. After the song ended, Joan sat down.

"So, to answer your question," Joan started. "I need to go back a few years. You see, our son Jason's startup company in the Research Triangle wasn't doing as well as he had hoped. They needed money, and investors were not backing them. The company was bleeding cash to stay afloat. So, Fabio and I've been heading to Durham every few weeks to help Jason's family with our time and money."

Susan frowned briefly, and Joan wondered whether her explanation was plausible. She hoped it would keep Susan from asking more questions. Perhaps she ought to let Fabio know how personal Susan's questions are getting, knowing Fabio wouldn't like that.

"So, how often have you and Fabio driven back and forth from North Carolina to The Villages in the past six months?" Susan asked.

"Why, who's counting? What difference does it make?" Joan snapped with quite some sarcasm in her voice.

Susan sat back and quietly said: "None, really. It just seems to be more and more often. I just hoped nothing was wrong because if there was, I figured you could confide in me and perhaps I could help out...."

Joan cut her off. "Don't worry. We're just fine," she said, finished her drink, and stood up.

"Okay, no problem then," Susan said and got up. She felt that she'd figured it wrong. Joan wasn't ready to talk. It had gotten a little chilly, and they walked over to the golf cart. Once inside, she closed up the plastic side covers and drove off while the Anita Drink Bank played its last evening tunes.

The conversation during the drive home was subdued, each preoccupied with their thoughts. They made some small talk, and as they got to the Spencer's house, Joan thanked Susan for a fun evening. Little did Susan know that Joan's head was spinning, hoping she hadn't given out any information that Fabio would get angry about later.

Chapter 11

Ocala Again

The next day, Susan reflected on the previous night. She was sure that Joan had not given an honest answer. There were just too many unexplained things. Joan never said anything about her granddaughter Ellie. The issue of helping someone like their son financially could be done via bank transfer or something like Venmo. And what about Jason's wife? Not a word about Erin. It bothered her that Joan and Fabio's comings and goings were, to put it simply, suspicious. Period. Joan had acted out of character at Spanish Springs: relaxed one minute and damn nervous the next. Now it was almost noon, and she hadn't seen Joan yet. Was she avoiding her again?

Susan was outside in the front yard, taking care of some plants. Fabio went to the mailbox, and Susan wanted to talk with him. Still, her neighbor turned around and quickly disappeared into the house. She stayed outside. Given the proximity of their homes, it wouldn't be the first time she could overhear what was being said at the Spencers when they raised their voices. Once

Fabio was inside, there was a sudden argument, and she took two steps closer to the house where Joan and Fabio were going at it quite loudly. It was clear they were arguing about moving. Nothing was said about their son Jason or where they might move to. She walked closer to their lanai, pretending to clip some leaves and small branches from a bush between their houses.

"How are we going to stop this? We are in so much trouble. Don't you realize that? You need to talk to the big boss or to the police!"

Susan kept clipping away.

"What? We can't go into a witness protection program! I'll meet with the guy in Ocala and pick up one more load. I'll go tomorrow tonight at 9:00 PM, and then we'll figure out what we'll do with the house. Damn it. This isn't going to be easy. And next time, stop talking to that woman next door!"

Susan froze. So, Joan must have told her husband about her questions last night. She smiled. It obviously had some effect. And more importantly, she was now sure that her neighbors were involved in something illegal. If she wanted to find out, there was only one way. Follow Fabio wherever he was going and see what he was up to. She heard a door slam, and the argument came to a halt.

The next evening, about twenty to 8:00 PM, Susan took a short walk on her street. She didn't want to miss Fabio leaving the house and made several more loops. On her third excursion, she saw Fabio in his garage, taking out his golf bag from the trunk of his Equinox SUV. He put a large black blanket in the back and closed the door. He never noticed her, and she backed her brand new KIA Optima out of her garage. She checked for all her selected accessories on the passenger seat: a bottle of water, her phone and a pair of binoculars. Tom had been an avid bird watcher and used them all the time. She was sure Fabio had never seen the car since she'd just bought it a few weeks ago. Her golf cart was all she'd driven since the Spencers had been down here. Fabio didn't know her car.

She drove up ahead toward the entrance to their village and parked. It was getting dark, and with her tinted windows, Fabio would never recognize who followed him. She waited another half hour to finally see Fabio leave and pass her. Thinking about the spy movies she'd seen, she thought she'd have to keep a safe distance and not follow him too closely. On the other hand, there were many lights on the main road. That would be tricky. She planned to get close to him once he parked to do whatever he would do.

Susan checked the time: 8:15 PM. After making the first turn, following Fabio about forty yards in front of her, she became nervous because it felt too close and varied her distance during the ride. Her curiosity grew as the ride continued, often reminding herself that she was to stay out of trouble and just watch. She'd let another car merge between their two vehicles a few times, but she kept a close eye on Fabio's vehicle. She made all the green and red lights together with him.

Driving into Ocala, Susan figured that this was Fabio's destination. He was making several quick turns using his blinkers promptly. Fabio turned into a deserted strip mall near the end of a long street. She decided to drive on as she'd be the only car there and slowly made a left turn at the intersection, keeping her eye on Fabio's car. Susan took an immediate left at the mall's top end and parked, immediately turning her lights off. She was glad she brought the binoculars because she was at least a hundred yards away from the spot where Fabio had parked.

She adjusted the focus when a dark sedan pulled up next to the Equinox. A stocky man got out of the car; Hispanic, she thought. He sported a mustache. All this looked like illicit business, and Susan felt her gut feeling was being confirmed. Fabio moved to the back of his car and opened the trunk. After he handed a single small package wrapped in what looked like black plastic, he took several gray packages from the man, putting them against the back seat. Fabio then covered them up with the blanket she'd seen earlier. Susan got out her phone and took a picture, zooming in as much as possible. It looked blurry, and she couldn't even make out the license plates. Still, she took a few more shots and saw Fabio closing the trunk. After that, there seemed to be a short discussion during which the Hispanic man raised his finger. Fabio got into his car and drove off.

Susan was stunned at what she'd seen. What was that all about? What was in the package Fabio gave the man, and what was in the boxes he got in return? Contraband? Money? Something else? Lots of thinking to do, she figured. Once the parking lot was clear, she drove off and stopped to get something small to eat. Whenever she was nervous, she needed to eat.

She stopped at Aneta's Bistro. Her mouth was watering for Aneta's famous pancakes and syrup. The carbs should calm down her nerves.

After paying the bill, Susan went home and got into bed, wondering if she should tell someone what she had witnessed this evening. She tossed and turned but finally fell into a troubled sleep.

Chapter 12

Moving Out

The house sold in two days. Fabio and Joan signed all the powers of attorney documents, so they didn't need to be present at the closing. This morning at five, movers from a small local company which they paid in cash, left with a small truck for a storage facility in Raleigh. Shortly after, the Spencers headed in the same direction without saying goodbye to their neighbors.

A few miles into the trip, Fabio glanced at his wife and saw that she was napping. He knew that she was happy with her whole plan being executed perfectly. According to her, all their problems were solved now. Their vacation would start with a flight at 7:00 PM from RDU. All their mail would be forwarded to the closing attorney's office. They'd drop off the last shipment because he had picked up several more packages the evening before in Ocala, spreading out the pick-ups, hoping to avoid suspicion because of regularity. Nobody knew what they were up to.

The packages were partly stashed in a suitcase, under seats and in shopping bags. Maybe they weren't proper hiding places, but anyone driving by wouldn't notice anything unusual. Fabio was still worried about the plan, but he'd gone along, so far, so good. He was amazed at how Joan had stepped up to it all. After all, once he contacted their guy, she was the one who wanted to have a talk with him and his boss. When she returned from her trip to Ocala, she told him that when these men said they couldn't quit now, at least not until they found someone else, Joan had feigned that she understood and that it was okay. That's why he had picked up the last package and pretended everything was fine. Their plan then came together quickly.

He had read that the chances of getting through unscathed on I-95 were excellent. He didn't want to jinx the trip by saying it was the last, and they never got stopped. Of course, as a driver, he had to avoid triggering a red flag. Before they even took their first trip with the goods, his contact told him that the chances of getting stopped increased when the driver was careless. He had recommended that they didn't drive a large sedan or drive with the windows cracked or open as if to signal that there were chemical odors inside. He wondered about that because they'd never smelled anything. During one of the conversations with their Durham contact, they learned that even the car's color was important. Light blue, beige and brown shades blend in better.

Of course, driving consistently below the speed limit or speeding and weaving in or out of lanes could appear odd to police, but so was erratic driving, which might draw the attention of law enforcement. Then there was the situation of what to do when pulled over. If you breathed heavily, were sweating nervously and avoided eye contact with the officer, you were waving red flags. Fabio knew that he wouldn't be able to handle it. He figured he'd exhibit all these things, so he drove carefully and paid attention. Except, for some reason, today, he felt extra nervous. This was their last run, nothing unusual as far as the load was concerned, but one just never knew.

Having reached I495 near Jacksonville, Joan sat up. "Wow, did I need that! Those few naps during the night were not enough."

"Same here, but that pot of coffee is doing the trick."

"Good. I can drive some if you want me to."

"I'm fine, dear. Just keep an eye out for state troopers. Traffic is getting worse. I think we hit rush hour here."

"Just be careful," Joan said and continued. "I'm so glad we could sell the house with most of the furniture to stay there."

"So am I. This really will keep our storage fees down. By the way, I don't think our neighbors know we've left. That was indeed a small white unmarked truck, just like we ordered."

"It was perfect. Even if someone had seen it, that person wouldn't have known it to be a moving truck. Also, we were lucky to sell quickly without ever putting up a for-sale sign."

"They'll find out soon enough, though. The neighbors, I mean."

"That's fine because it gives us a head start on our vacation. I can't wait. When they notice that we're gone, they'll figure we're on another two to three-week trip to our place in the Arbors."

Fabio nodded and didn't answer. He still had to make that drop in Durham, which made him uneasy. What if he was given another present to take to Florida? He'd have to keep it if he took it, and the boss would have another reason to track them down. He'd better have a good reason if he didn't take it. He hadn't thought of one yet, and it bothered him. Then there was the fact that they wouldn't be paid for the current trip. They'd decided that this was fine. They regarded this last trip as their ticket out of the rut. He checked the time and estimated their regular breakfast site was only an hour away. Perfect time for a coffee refill, he figured.

***

Fabio paid the bill and ensured the lid of his coffee cup was tight. "That should get me to Durham," he said and sighed. "I hope we don't have an incident on the way home," he said.

"Why are you suddenly worried?" Joan asked, grabbing her purse and sliding out of the booth.

"I have this feeling that it's all been too perfect. I'm not sure why, but it annoys me to think something will happen."

"Well, the boss and his gang won't be on to us. So, nothing can happen from that side. Are you worried about an accident or being stopped by a trooper?"

"Exactly that," he said and paused briefly. "And what if someone was keeping an eye on us and somehow, we are stopped at the airport so we can't leave?"

"You really worry too much. Everything will be fine. Remember, we're not even going to our house at the Arbors. Straight to the airport. Nobody will have seen us leave, and nobody will see us arrive. Those neighbors will figure that we're still in Florida while we actually will have disappeared."

"I hope you're right. But before the airport, we have to make the drop, which will be the first time we do this late afternoon or early evening. It may look suspicious."

"You'll come up with some excuse. Why don't you call the contact now and tell him we'll be dropping it all off at 4:30. Tell him we have a family emergency and must spend all evening away."

"I've already thought about something like that. The one thing remains: what happens when he gives us a box with money again?"

"Easy. Same reason. I'll tell the guy I have to park our car in an unsafe area. I'll suggest picking the money up before our next trip down. He'll buy that."

"I hope he does. All right then. Let's get back on the road. We don't want to miss our flight."

Chapter 13

The Lecture

The Health and Wellness Club had reserved the largest possible room at Piedmont Hall. They expected over a hundred people to attend an OLLI class led by Dr. Veekar Gupta. The evening subject was announced via the community bulletin as "Living Without Opioids." The organizers in the club were well aware that it was a topic of much-needed discussion, with many people undergoing painful procedures and needing relief from pain.

Joe Malinski had signed up right away. In his years with the New York Police and Vice Squad, drugs had been the main reason for most crimes. As a detective, he usually dealt with the results of those crimes: homicides. Finding illicit drugs and the dealers were left to the NARC units. Today, however, he was keen on finding out what forms drugs took these days and how they added to the increase in the greater Durham area's crime level. Of course, he knew of several people taking painkillers for whatever reason. However, he had no evidence of large-scale misuse of these drugs, especially opioids. Added to the prolific use of laced drugs, he felt that he should be better informed. This lecture would set him straight, and who knows, one day, he might use the information to help someone. Maybe he'd even contact that detective. Yes, Vinder was his name; he also lived in the community.

The meeting was indeed well-attended and was starting on time. The speaker gave just enough background and history on the use of painkillers and opioids. He then explained the progression of using ibuprofen and aspirin to more potent drugs. Often that's when the addiction began. Much time was spent introducing Fentanyl into the mix, and the staggering death rate when laced with opioids. Fentanyl was mixed with heroin and legal drugs. That's where drug dealers came in, and that's what Joe wanted to learn about.

Dr. Gupta switched over to the figures for Durham County. It was hard to fully understand how the COVID19 pandemic affected the county's opioid-related fatalities because the data only covered part of 2020. He said that the county's trend followed a similar trend in the country. The number of opioid overdose deaths has significantly increased. As various numbers and graphs were being shown, Joe reflected on one of his neighbors who had undergone emergency gallbladder surgery four years ago. After a while, the man realized that the prescribed opioids didn't do the trick. He was given 30 milligrams of Oxycodone followed by 80 milligrams of Oxycontin two years later. Joe had heard from the man's wife that he had changed doctors several times. He had a good idea why that was the case.

As if planned, Dr. Gupta covered the issue of 'doctor-shopping' to get more pills. The insurance would pay for one prescription, and the other was paid in cash. But this kind of shopping was becoming riskier, and in many cases, the insurance company would stop paying altogether. North Carolina has passed several laws to combat the opioid epidemic, requiring prescribers to receive training and abide by a nationally recognized opioid abuse screening method. A law was passed limiting the number of days supply of an opioid could be prescribed.

Joe had a good idea about how his neighbor had become dependent on opioids and how he was getting his drugs. Once the meds were no longer available in a legitimate way and limited at that, it left those dependent on opioids to find other sources. He heard the speaker mention that some people turned to cheaper heroin, more potent than synthetic drugs. He suspected that even more people turned to illicit drugs during the pandemic since many medical providers were unavailable or saw fewer patients.

Dr. Gupta explained that for 2020, the preliminary data showed that prescription opioids were not the most common drugs involved in overdose deaths for the first time in twenty years. Increased misuse of illegal opioids laced with Fentanyl played a significant role in the rise of overdoses. Joe understood that street Fentanyl was a synthetic opioid several times more potent than the legally manufactured form of the drug.

He was trying to comprehend how people in his neighborhood would get these Fentanyl-laced drugs. His neighbor was currently at a detox facility, and he hadn't heard of any overdoses in the community. Perhaps an exception in the statistics of the county and the state? Then again, who would openly admit that this is how a senior citizen died in the retirement community?

The presentation switched to various ways of getting harmful drugs into our county. Joe was well aware of the smuggling of drugs, from marijuana to laced opioids, from Miami to New York. I-95 was known as the drug corridor. With over 200,000 vehicles using it daily, law enforcement faced the impossible task of stopping the flow of drugs. While he was in New York, smugglers were never caught on the road; most arrests were made at drop-off points or where large deals went down. The couriers were hardly ever caught. Over the years, the I-95 trunk grew branches to ever-growing communities along the east coast. Durham was one such location on a short branch west.

The question and answer session lasted almost as long as the presentation. Neighbors were concerned about how to know they were using a legal drug, could all pharmacies be trusted and what if you ran out and a friend gave you their drugs? Almost every question diverged into statements that started with "I have a friend who...." Joe wondered how many people were talking about themselves. He wondered how much of this social calamity had infiltrated his own community. He felt ill at ease.

Chapter 14

Mary

Mary Valero felt she found heaven when a friend introduced her to Carolina Arbors. An "Active Adult Community" with social clubs, a huge gym, and shady wooded trails for cycling, walking, and her favorite - birdwatching. She was often introduced as "the Italian lady with the binoculars" at parties and club events. Her binoculars hung on a hook with her keys and always traveled with her out the door. She walked the trails, over the bridges, and by the waterfalls, always with binoculars handy to see how many bird species she could spot.

And, of course, she also favored the wine club, where she could showcase her talent for Italian cooking and fine Italian wines. Her zaftig shape supported the axiom of not trusting a skinny cook. The move to CA was also the perfect opportunity for her to escape the "good intentions" of her huge raucous family in New York and all their disastrous match-making attempts after two failed marriages.

Even though Mary had sworn off romantic relationships after her second divorce, one of her neighbors, Joe Malinski, had caught her eye as he jogged by her kitchen window on his way to the trail every morning. If Mary was home, she was in the kitchen. Her heart had skipped a beat.

She knew that Joe was a retired New York cop whose beat was Brooklyn. He seemed like a good guy and was in great shape, tall and lanky, and quite the golfer from the word at the clubhouse. He also attended some of the wine club events and rescued Mary a few weeks back after she got a bit tipsy. Joe made sure she got home safe and sound. Such a gentleman; perhaps she should make him a good Italian 'thank-you' dinner.

Then there were her other neighbors: Fabio and Joan. A while back, humming an oldie she heard at Piedmont Hall after a meeting, Mary headed to the mailbox kiosks to gather her mail when the couple pulled up. They parked their silver Buick sedan in the driveway. "Hi there; welcome home. That was a quick trip," Mary called out and noticed Fabio looking annoyed. He ran for the front door and disappeared into the house. The garage door opened, and he parked the car inside. The door closed quickly after that. *Such weird behavior,* Mary had thought.

Entering her home, she shook her head and mumbled to herself; *I wonder why they even bought a house here? Of all the people to move next to – those are some strange ones. They spend most of their time in the Villages and surely don't socialize with anyone. Their blinds were always shut tight, and even when home, they never even came to a block party.* Mary continued to ponder the strangeness of her next-door neighbors as she let her dark shoulder-length hair loose from its scrunchie and scrutinized her gray roots. "Time to hit the bottle," she said aloud, walking into the kitchen and adding *Hair Color* to her lengthy shopping list. She decided on a quick shower and then a trip to Harris Teeter.

She remembered distinctly that the next day after returning from playing crazy canasta, Mary saw Fabio backing out of his garage and wondered where he was going without Joan. They had everything delivered, groceries, pharmacy, Amazon, Fed Ex and UPS daily. She had never seen her neighbors one without the other. *Something isn't right here*, she thought. *Call me a nosy neighbor, but I'm going to follow him; maybe I can pretend to run into him at a store.* She hopped into her car and drove behind the Equinox to TW Alexander and then onto US-70, heading for Durham. Fabio turned into an empty parking lot behind a strip mall with weeds and rusty garbage bins. *This is a strange place for a romantic interlude,* Mary wondered as she parked across the street, grabbing her binoculars from her purse. Her heart was racing; *if Fabio spotted her, how could she explain her presence? What in the world is going on?*

Fabio had pulled up next to a sporty-looking car. Mary adjusted the binoculars to get a good look at the man in the car. He wore a hoodie, so she couldn't make out his face. Something fishy was going on. Where at first she thought there was a secret meeting with a woman perhaps, she now was sure that this was a hand-off involving something illegal. Fabio took smaller, tightly wrapped packages from cardboard boxes and handed them to his contact. After emptying every box, Fabio looked around as if wary of any onlookers. Mary quickly drew in her breath and dropped the binoculars on her lap. *I better get out of here quickly before he sees me. What were Joan and Fabio up to? What kind of crazy game are they playing?*

Chapter 15

A Chance Meeting

The day had gone as planned. Once their car was parked at a cheaper off-site location away from the airport, Fabio and Joan high-fived it in the back seat of the Uber car. They hadn't done this in a long time, but now it felt like they needed to.

"Kudos to Joan, the planner!" Fabio said with a smile.

"And thanks for getting us here safely," she answered.

"Thank God our contact was understanding and that last delivery went lickety-split."

They didn't seem to care that the driver was listening. They didn't say anything revealing and had practiced that many times before. They both understood, and that was sufficient.

Fabio took out their suitcases at the airport, and Joan carried their two carry-ons. They thanked the driver and were ready to enter the terminal when they loud and clearly heard, "Hi, neighbors. Good to see you. Didn't know you were back!"

They automatically snapped their heads in the direction of the person yelling. Fabio immediately thought this was a mistake, but it was too late. His surprised look changed into a bit of a grin: "Mary, funny seeing you here. Are you flying out?"

Mary stepped closer, resting her hand on the top of her car. "No, I wish! I just dropped someone off. Where are you two heading? Really, I didn't know you were back."

Fabio was quicker than Joan, who was about to say something. "Oh, we just flew up for the day. Had to see our granddaughter. You understand. We're on our way back to Florida now."

Joan stared at her husband. She had to do some quick thinking. "That's right," she blurted out. Just an up and down, you know. Everything okay at the house?"

"Yes, sure. When are you coming up next?"

"In a few weeks," Fabio said, wheeling the suitcases toward the terminal. Joan followed his lead.

"Okay then," Mary said. Have a safe trip back. Are you flying to Orlando?"

"Yes," Joan said and waved. "See you soon!"

Mary got into her car as they disappeared behind the second sliding door.

"Well, that was a close one," Joan said. "Phew!"

"You can say that again. What are the chances?"

"I think we did well. You did some quick thinking there. I knew what you were getting at."

"I could tell. Anyway, let's get out of here before we meet more neighbors," Fabio laughed.

The line at check-in was short, and soon they had their boarding tickets in hand. It was a short flight to Charlotte, but Joan figured they were out of here.

"Maybe we should have driven to Charlotte and left the car there," Fabio remarked as they worked their way to the TSA area.

"What do you mean?"

"Suppose these guys come along and talk to Mary, and she says we flew back to Florida, and then they check things out, and it turns out we went to Charlotte."

"So?" Joan asked. "First of all, dear, she'll tell them we went to Florida, and they would have to do some serious hacking in computers to find out where we really went. Secondly, remember, we booked separate tickets for tomorrow morning to St. Maarten. That makes it harder to find us."

Fabio shrugged his shoulders. "All right then, let's get our driver's licenses and go through security."

***

Later that night, at the hotel near the Charlotte Airport, Fabio set the alarm on his phone for 7:00 AM. Instead of going out, they skipped dinner and bought a sandwich in the lobby's small shop. Staying in their room would lessen the chance of running into someone they knew, he had jokingly said to his wife.

"So, I arranged a shuttle at eight, which gives us plenty of time for our 10:00 AM flight then," he said.

"Fine with me. I can't wait," Joan said and got into bed. "You know," she continued, "I feel such a relief I can almost cry. The last two weeks were hard on us. I can't wait to experience the Caribbean beaches."

"Yes, you're right. I hope we sleep well and get some needed rest. It has been a hell of a long day."

Chapter 16

Mary's Suspicion

Later that evening, Mary thought about the chance encounter. It was so unusual for Joan and Fabio to fly to Florida. She knew they were frugal. She swore she'd seen Fabio put keys in his pocket, perhaps his car keys. Did they drive? Maybe he wanted to ensure he had the keys to their car at the Orlando Airport. She shook her head as sometimes she really couldn't figure them out. She swore she'd seen them leave about three weeks ago, and they were back already and were going back right away.

She couldn't shake the feeling that, besides the travel back and forth, the frequency was increasing, and it had to be more than just coming over to help their son's family. They must know I-95 so well that they'd know the best rest stops and restaurants. Having planned a road trip to Key West in the Fall, she'd have to ask them. For now, it bothered her that they went to Florida with the possibility that their car was in North Carolina. She knew from Joan that they'd sold their golf cart, and you need at least a golf cart to get around. Well, maybe they are using a friend's cart, or their car was indeed waiting for them in Orlando. Why would one put keys away at this airport if one's car was at another airport?

It was about two days later when she gathered the Spencers' mail. She was allowed to throw out junk mail, so she went through all the pieces before discarding or throwing them into a large paper bag she kept from shopping at Harris Teeter nearby. A letter from a Florida real estate company piqued her interest. It was a business-size envelope, and the address was hand-written. In red letters, the word URGENT was underlined a few times. Once back in the house, she decided to call Joan to ask her whether she should forward the piece to their address in Florida. She left a message.

She tried to reach Joan a few times a day during the next few hours, but there was no answer. It was very odd, and Mary grew even more concerned when she made one more call. She heard a message that the message folder was full. She was almost sure she had Fabio's cell number somewhere but couldn't find it. Finally, she decided to contact the real estate company. A quick Google search got her a number. Her call was answered immediately, and she dove right in.

"Hi, I got a letter a few days ago from you. It was for my neighbors, Fabio and Joan Spencer, who live in The Villages. It's marked urgent, and I haven't been able to reach them as they went to their home there days ago. Can you help me out?"

There was a slight hesitation at the other end. "Let me check with an agent; please hold on," the person said.

Mary was patient and waited until the woman returned and spoke right away. "The agent says to forward it to their address in The Villages."

"It was marked URGENT in red. I'm not sure whether this is time-sensitive information, but this will take another week to get there," Mary objected.

"Let me check again," the person sighed.

This time it was an agent who came on the line. "Hi, you said it was for a Mr. and Mrs. Spencer?"

"Yes, I'm their neighbor in Durham, where they have another home."

"I'll check with some other agents and a few real estate teams here," the agent stated. "Can I call you back?"

Mary provided her number and stared at the envelope on the counter. Something was fishy here, she thought. If they do business with an agent in Florida, why didn't the mail go to their address there? This didn't make any sense. It crossed her mind that perhaps they'd sell their house there and move to the Carolina Arbors for good. Was that the reason they flew to Orlando?

Mary shook her head and asked aloud: "Wait, are there even direct flights to Orlando from RDU?" Killing some time, she checked on her laptop. She quickly found a direct flight with Delta at 7:45 every evening. Why was she suddenly so suspicious of the Spencers? It was weird that she never saw any signs of them being home when she spotted them at the airport. Perhaps they lied? Did they not fly to Orlando that evening? They seemed very surprised to have run into her, and the story by Fabio about visiting their ailing granddaughter appeared out of character. They usually spend days at Ellie's bed, either at home or in the hospital. Was something wrong there, and they weren't ready to share? So many questions, Mary sighed.

Her phone rang about an hour later; it was a real estate agent. "Hi, Mary? This is Angie Madden. You called about my letter to the Spencers?"

"Yes, I did. Thanks for calling back. I tried to reach Joan, but nobody picked up, and now the message box is full."

"I know what you mean; it happened to me too."

"So, what should I do with the letter? They told me they weren't coming back here for several weeks."

"That's odd," Angie said slowly. "They sold their home here in The Villages, and we forgot we needed one more signature. I tried a DocuSign via email but got no response from either Mr. or Mrs. Spencer."

"Well, I'd say they're incommunicado then," Mary concluded. "Should I just hang on to the letter until they show up here? Since they no longer have a house there, I expect them here."

"I don't think we have another option," the agent agreed. "It's just that we need their signatures at the closing next week. Do let me know if you see them or get in touch with them. No need to do anything with the letter for now. Thanks for reaching out, Mary. Have a good day."

Mary let all that sink in a little. Now she was sure they weren't flying to Orlando that evening. What the hell? Selling their home in Florida? Maybe on vacation in Orlando, but that didn't make much sense given where they lived for so long. For that matter, they may be on vacation somewhere totally different and didn't want to share. Perhaps they are out of the country. But why would they lie? More questions were coming.

That evening, Mary watched a video recording of an OLLI lecture from a few days ago. She hadn't been able to attend. The quality was reasonable, and she'd at least watch the presentation. The Q&A may take too much time. She listened to Dr. Gupta, and she was fascinated. She'd been a nurse for 42 years, and the pain drugs landscape was just unbelievable. She was aware of all the illicit drugs and witnessed the consequences of laced drugs and overdose - quite the evolution over time. She couldn't believe that people would act as couriers, jeopardizing their future if caught. Then again, maybe the chance of being stopped and searched was small. Anyway, who would do that?

She dropped onto her sofa and covered her mouth with her hand.

Chapter 17

Dinner with Joe

Thank goodness for the trails. Mary smiled, remembering her evening walk yesterday and her chance encounter with Joe. He seemed very upbeat, and they walked and talked all the way back to their street, providing her the opportunity to invite him for that homemade Italian dinner. "I thought you'd never ask," he had replied with a huge smile.

It was a beautiful spring evening for dinner on the porch. Setting an inviting table for two on the private patio under a trellis draped with Carolina jasmine and twinkle lights, Mary hummed to Italian cooking music, compliments of Pandora, softly entertaining her through her open windows. She loved spring and a chance to open the windows and enjoy as much fresh air as possible before that awful yellow pollen arrived. She was pleased by surveying her table setting to ensure it looked casual and not too romantic. A bit of romance would surely be welcomed.

The evening went well. A colorful antipasto was a hit, followed by her special veal scallopini, fettucini, and a bottle of her favorite Pino Noir. Joe relaxed in his chair as Mary cleared the dishes to make room for dessert. The conversation had hit a dead spot, and Joe hated that. He talked briefly about their HOA board and continuing regulations regarding the pandemic until Mary had cleaned some dishes.

"How about a little walk before dessert," Joe suggested. A beautiful sunset blazed across the horizon as they wound their way down to the trail, walking quietly. A rustling in the woods caught their attention, and Joe pointed out a deer and fawn in the distance. "Such a peaceful sight," Mary said softly, not wanting to disturb the pair. "Speaking of peaceful, it's been tranquil over at our neighbors, the Spencers. Did you see them about three days ago? Apparently, they came up for a day. At least, that's what Fabio said when I ran into them at the airport."

"They are a strange pair," Joe added. Mary pointed to a bench, "Can we sit for a bit? There is something I'd like to discuss with you." Making certain no one else was around, Mary asked a single question. "What can you tell me about drug smugglers from Florida to perhaps here in Durham?"

"Wow, Mary, it sounds like you may have some information and concerns. That business of being involved in it could pose a dangerous situation. You know, I've been interested in the opioid problem here ever since five years ago. The Durham police came to discuss the interstate distribution of drugs through this area." Joe explained what he knew about drug trafficking along the I-95 corridor. "Drugs pour into south Florida from South America and the Caribbean. The interstate is a 2,000 -mile highway that goes all the way to Houlton, Maine. It has many names, such as Cocaine Alley and Cocaine Lane. In the seventies and eighties, it was called the Reefer Express.

Nowadays, Cocaine, Heroin, Fentanyl, and Oxy get transported, mostly by car, along what was once a colonial mail route. If you obey the speed limit and drive a nondescript car, the goods will get through ninety-nine out of a hundred times. With increased law enforcement efforts, the transporters have gotten very creative, hiding the goods in door panels, behind glove compartments and anywhere a nook and cranny is found."

"I used to think our community had nothing to do with this, but that was until yesterday." Mary took a deep breath. "I sure don't want to get in the middle of anything like that," Mary said.

'Sounds like you know more about it than you are saying. Why don't you want to get in the middle of anything? Tell me. I'm an ex-detective, remember? It's not like I'll arrest anyone," Joe smiled.

Mary hesitated but then shared her observations and hunches with Joe. She told him that one evening at dusk, she saw Fabio in a bad part of Durham. He gave several boxes to someone with a Camaro. At first, she thought that was odd, but then she saw a sign for a Goodwill store. She had never asked him about it, but she felt she had to mention it to Joe after what she'd figured out last night. When she was finished, Joe nodded. He had put his hand on her arm because she seemed to shake.

"Let's take a step back before we make any accusations, but from what you have told me, I have to agree that there is a concern. It's like they say: *where there's smoke, there's fire.*"

Mary nodded and took a deep breath.

"Let's head back to that cannoli, Mary," Joe said. "I don't want to scare you, but best to let the professionals deal with it if anything is going on. You need to focus on those wonderful meals – that was excellent!" Joe smiled down at his new friend.

They finished dessert without a further discussion about Fabio and Joan. As Mary began clearing the table, Joe took his leave. But not without a sweet thank you hug and kiss on her cheek. A charming grin adorned her face the rest of the evening.

Chapter 18

The Drop Point

Joe was impressed with the things Mary had divulged to him. Of course, it figured that the constant flow of illegal drugs from Florida and Texas made it up north. The fact that couriers could be any person, regardless of age, background, or whatever, made sense. Why not? Money was the lubricant that greased the wheel of many things: business, organized crime, and individuals. He'd seen it all in his days on the force in New York City. The smallfolk were among hundreds of cogs in the wheels that relied on greasing.

Mary's suspicion, so well conveyed to him, gnawed at him a little. Yes, he met the Spencers many times and conversed with Fabio. Except for the frequent travels to Florida, everything seemed to be above board. Joe had enough smarts, though, mainly accumulated during his forty years with law enforcement, to realize that sometimes things are not necessarily what they seemed. The locations, the frequency, and the secret rendezvous at dark and hidden areas all indicated that something was afoot. The more he had listened to Mary, the stronger he felt the red flags popping into his mind. He decided a little investigation was in order while the couple was off to wherever they claimed to be traveling.

The next day, Joe left the house at about 8:30 PM. He was still eating the last piece of his Jersey Mike's sub and had suddenly found the urge to go to downtown Durham. The location Mary had given him was easy enough to find. She mentioned every street and turn, so he drove there in less than twenty minutes. The dark parking lot of interest was on his right as only a faint light came from a small window in a restaurant or the store's back door. He drove to the end of the block, turned around, and parked on the other side of the street, where he had a good view of the lot. He didn't expect anything to happen, but he wanted to view the place and figure out how a large drug package could exchange hands at that location. He was almost sure there wouldn't be any cameras. Any drug handler would have looked for that.

Several garbage containers sat against walls, and a fair amount of litter was strewn across the lot. An empty lot at that, since there were no cars parked. He did see the 'Tow Away' sign when he drove by. The only people that would park there would be employees. He noticed that it was past 9:00 PM. Most likely, the lights he saw were not from a bar or restaurant after all. Those would still be open. He tried to picture this now-empty lot the time Mary followed Fabio. According to her, Fabio had pulled in and backed up against a brick wall sporting a large white Nike shoe advertisement. Whoever parked and walked to the back of the car would be shielded from the street by one of the large green garbage bins shoved against that wall. Mary said that minutes later, a vehicle she identified as a Camero had pulled up and performed the same maneuver, parking next to Joan's SUV. For Mary to have seen what he now imagined, she must have parked about where he was now. Mary had described the muscle car as being black. She couldn't say more about the man since his hoody obscured his face, and it was dark outside. This wasn't much to go on, but perhaps a short walk to the spot near the wall wouldn't hurt. He left his car and locked it. Looking left and right, he safely crossed the street. There were no walkers, and it all seemed very quiet. Once he got on the other side of the first trash container, he put latex gloves on and crouched down. He figured it was very likely that some transaction had happened here yesterday. The Spencers had returned and gone straight to the airport. That means that if they had contraband, they had to get rid of it first. But that was last night. He stared at the surface, and besides bits of paper, wood and a few glistening things, probably broken pieces of glass, nothing was noteworthy. Not that he expected to find any pills of any sort. He walked back and forth.

Still, transferring stuff from an SUV to a much smaller Camero puzzled him. It was like downsizing. Then, he realized what must have happened. He opened the container that shielded him from the street and looked inside. Bingo! Five or more cardboard boxes. He grabbed the top one and turned it to all sides until he saw what he was looking for. Clearly, stuck on the box was a UPS label. He took out his phone and turned on its light. "I've got you," he smiled. There it was. The address of the Spencers in Florida and Fabio's name! His hunch proved correct: they'd been at this location last night. The boxes were probably stuffed with smaller items because the size of the box led him to figure that by itself, it was too large to squeeze into the backseat or trunk of a Camaro. He briefly pondered what to do with the box but threw it back in after taking a picture of the label. He grabbed the next box, a smaller one. He smelled the inside. Not recognizing anything, he expected to see a label again, but there was none this time. Looking back inside, he noticed a small sticker with a handwritten number: 1200. He also took a picture of that. The third box had an Amazon label. Its contents had been sent to the Spencers in The Villages. Another shot, another box, he figured. As he took that box, he looked around. He was still all alone. The third box was a bit strange. It had been wrapped in brown paper, partially torn away from the top. He peeled away the remaining paper and quickly found that it was a used box again. Looking at the label, partially removed, he smiled. This was an Ocala address in Florida. Only part of the last name was shown, and the tear had also ripped the number before the street name. He had enough. After his last picture, he closed the container. He scratched his head: judging by the size of the boxes, the Spencers must have brought up about twenty kilos. He estimated that to be about 12,000 to an astounding 20,000 pills. He had little time to act now and headed home as he couldn't wait to call detective Vinder.

All the way home, he felt like he had years ago, still on the force. The adrenalin rush primed by the belief that he was on to something that may solve a case had hit him hard. His hand trembled as he unlocked the garage door to the hallway leading to the kitchen. From a stuffed drawer, he retrieved the detective's card. His previous encounters with Travis Vinder had been professional, and he felt a little proud that he had been helpful in the case of the murder of one of the members of the men's club. He knew Vinder would get this ball rolling.

The phone rang at the other end, and Travis answered. "Vinder, homicide."

"Detective Vinder, Joe here, Joe Malinski."

"Ah, yes. Joe. From the neighborhood, right?"

"Yes. Listen, I wanted to talk to you about something. Do you have a minute?"

Travis was quick to respond. "Sure, what's on your mind?"

"I've investigated whether some of my neighbors are drug couriers. I know that this isn't your beat, but I believe they are hauling God knows what illegal stuff from Florida. Who would I contact there at the station? Can you get me in touch with someone?"

"Wow, Joe, really? From our Carolina Arbors neighborhood? I'm a bit surprised. But you're right: this is not my thing. How about I have someone call you in a little while? I got your number."

"Great. I'd like to share what I have found. Your chief will want to stop that kind of trafficking, maybe even roll up the whole gang in Durham."

"That would be the plan, I guess," Travis said. "Thanks for the call and the tip, Joe. Bye for now."

Joe stood with his back against the wall during the short call. He walked back to his car. Something about the best-laid plans and what happens to them came to mind.

Chapter 19

Evidence

After an hour without a return call, Joe gave up. More than likely, Vinder hadn't been able to get in touch with the other detective. It could easily be the following day, he figured. No point in staying here. He decided to make a second trip with the intent to remove at least one box of evidence, just in case the trash was to be collected in the morning. He drove back to the lot, and everything was like he had left. After taking several pictures, he wore his gloves again and grabbed one of the boxes with the Spencers' Florida address. He tossed the empty box in the back of his car and drove off. He checked his phone several times. Since it was after 11:00 PM, he didn't expect to get a callback. He wished Vinder had shared the name of the other detective with him.

He pulled into his driveway after opening the garage door with his remote. Mary was standing to the left side of the garage and waved briefly. He wondered what was up. Why was she still up? Did she find out more, or was she just curious about what he had found? He drove into the garage but left the box in the trunk. He walked outside.

"Hey Mary, up late?"

"C'mon, Joe, it's barely past eleven," she smiled. "So, what did you find?"

"How did you know I was looking for something."

"Joe, I know you. You were a great detective, and after what I told you, I just know that you were itching to go out there and check out that parking lot. So, did you find anything?"

Joe smiled. "Let's talk inside," he said.

They walked through the garage and the hallway and sat at the kitchen table.

"I know you found something! Drugs?" Mary asked impatiently. "You can tell me."

"Slow down a bit, Mary," Joe grinned. "Yes, I did go there, about the same time you did that day."

"And, did you see the guy with the Camaro?"

"I'm sure he only shows up when there's a drop-off. Tonight that was obviously not the case."

"Perhaps they did a few nights ago. I mean..." Mary started.

"You're clever. That's exactly what I figured. Coming back from Florida empty-handed was probably not an option. The fact that they didn't go home was a clue. You figured it well."

"So they did have a car here, after all."

"It may have been a rental, but that would be expensive driving it all the way from Florida."

"At any rate, another drop has been made."

"And, I do have a question. When you witnessed the drop that one time, what was Fabio handing over to the guy with the Camero?"

"I told you, small packages he had brought in boxes."

"Right, but how big were they?"

"I think they were all the same; I mean the packages. They were all about the size of a six-pack of beer. Why?"

"So, he just put them straight into the car from his SUV?"

"No, they were in cardboard boxes. Why is this important?" Mary asked, a little exasperated.

"Ah, yes. It was essential because what you witnessed was probably their standard packaged boxes, neatly sealed and not too heavy."

"And you think that's not what happened a few nights ago?"

"Indeed. I think the Spencers used any boxes they could find, putting several small packages into a larger box. And..." Mary interrupted Joe.

"And what? They left something behind, didn't they?"

"Mary, I was just about to tell you. Are you sure you weren't a detective in your earlier life?" Joe joked, cocking his head, smiling.

"No, but I watch a lot of crime series, and you start to get the idea of how these guys work, right?" she asked.

"Well, I'll tell you. In this case, they discarded boxes that the drug boxes came in."

"And you found them! Where, in the dumpster?"

"Yes," Joe sighed. "In the trash container."

"Did you bring them back?"

"That would be tampering with evidence. You get that right?"

"What if the dumpster is emptied early in the morning? Goodby evidence!"

"Okay, Mary, you got me. Yes, I took one box with a label on it. Don't share that with anyone."

"Oh, I wouldn't, Joe," Mary smiled. "That's our secret. Now, where's the box?"

"In my car. I'm leaving it there. It may have fingerprints, although it's probably Fabio's only, which doesn't prove very much."

"Did you call the police?" she asked, eyes wide open.

"Calm down, Mary. Yes, I called, and they'll call me back. And I didn't leave my prints, but I have pictures of all the boxes."

"Great," Mary laughed, twirling her right index finger in the air. "That could be days, Joe."

"I'll call back in the morning if that detective hasn't called me back by nine. Anyway, it was kind of careless for them to leave the shipping labels still stuck on the boxes," he said, grinning from ear to ear.

"They were that stupid, huh? It was their address, right?" she asked, sitting at the edge of her seat.

"Of course," Joe said and pulled up one picture, clearly showing their name and address in The Villages.

"They can arrest them right now," she said.

"On what charge? Throwing away a few boxes in a dumpster? I don't think so."

"Don't they have those sniffing dogs who can smell if drugs have been in those boxes?"

"That wouldn't do it either, Mary. Many things get thrown in dumpsters, and items quickly become contaminated."

"So, what's your next step, detective?" she asked teasingly.

"Easy. I'm done. That detective will have to take over. There're many things he'll have to verify, of course. Unfortunately, your initial suspicion, hunches and our suppositions don't hold up well in court. The boxes will only pan out if all the other pieces fall together."

"Oh, I get that. I do belong to our Thursday Afternoon Sleuths book club. Do you want me to give Vinder a call?"

"I've already called him. He's the one who told me another detective would call me back," Joe said as he got up, ready to leave. "Once I have briefed that detective, I'm sure he'll be in touch with you. Anyway, so it sounds like you know Vinder as well."

"Well, I wouldn't say that," Mary smiled. "Let's just say we've already helped him solve three murders."

Joe shook his head and laughed. "Hah, sleuths..."

Chapter 20

Jason's Story

Detective Malcolm Jackson stood in front of the Spencers home, listening to Joe Malinski. Mary watched from a distance in her driveway. She was glad that the detective had driven up in an unmarked car. There was no reason to get the whole neighborhood to see what the police were doing there.

"Vinder told me some sketchy things about your suspicions and what you found."

"Right," Joe said. "What are you doing about the possible evidence in the dumpster."

"Oh, I got some uniforms checking it out. They'll collect the items in the picture which you sent to Vinder. They'll bring them to the station. This is not a case yet, so I'm not sure it will get into the evidence room. So far, no crime had been committed."

"I get all that, detective," Joe said. "Once you have a case, those boxes will immediately become evidence," Joe said, walking toward his open garage.

"True," Jackson said. "Is there anything else? Don't tell me you picked something up from the scene?"

"I wasn't sure whether they picked up garbage downtown this morning. That would leave your uniforms empty-handed, right?"

"Damn, I didn't think of that," Jackson said, taking out his phone. "Let me call. Hold on."

Seconds later, he shook his head. "Bad luck, they did pick it up, and we're not about to go and check out the dump. But, is my suspicion correct, that maybe you were ahead of me here?"

Joe smiled, put on gloves and opened the trunk of his car. "Here you go: one telling box. This one is in one of the pictures I sent to Vinder."

"Well, in this case, I'm glad you moved the evidence, Joe. I'm not sure it will help us in the long run, but at least it's an argument for questioning the Spencers on how one of their boxes ended up in a dumpster, seven miles from home."

As Joe grabbed the box, the detective opened the back seat door of his sedan, and the box was now official evidence.

"So, let me get this straight," Jackson continued. "Your neighbors made many trips to Florida and back. There's a suspicion that a few nights ago, they went somewhere, but not to Florida because they sold their home there. Another neighbor witnessed a drop-off because she was suspicious, but she didn't know what was transacted. She didn't observe the last drop-off, but you found boxes in which they probably packed small packages of illegal drugs." He paused and rubbed his chin. "Vinder told me you're a retired detective from the City. You should know then that's not much to go on. A lot of circumstantial things, Joe."

Joe sighed. "Well, let's look at it from a different angle. The Spencers have a son Jason who lives nearby. I believe he moved to Morrisville. He may know where his parents are. Can't hurt to check with him. If he's concerned, you can try to find out where they went. Obviously, they have to come back here soon since they no longer have a home in Florida."

Jackson looked at his watch. "Do you know where he works?"

"I don't remember, but Mary over there may know," Joe said, motioning with his head towards his friend.

The detective waved Mary over. She didn't hesitate.

"I'm Mary Valero," she said. "What can I help you with, detective?"

"Would you happen to know where the Spencers' son works?"

"I have that in the house. Give me a sec."

Mary returned with a handwritten index card. "Here you go, detective. Jason Spencer, Chief Technology Officer at Sonic Security Systems."

"Thanks, Mary," Jackson smiled, and he took the card. "Oh, you even have an address. Well, I guess I'll pay him a visit. He may clear some things up. It can't hurt, and I'll put your minds at ease when I find out everything's okay."

Jackson returned to his car and drove off immediately, leaving Mary and Joe staring at him.

"Well, that was short," Mary said, touching Joe's arm. "Did you get the impression he doesn't think anything serious is going on?"

"It may have sounded like it, but you know what? If he thought there was no case here, he wouldn't have sent police to check out those boxes or have driven off to their son's business in Research Triangle Park," Joe said, taking Mary's hand. "You'll see; he'll be back because I don't think Jason will have all the answers, right or wrong."

"Ah, you're so confident."

"Let's go have a cup of coffee at my house," Joe said.

***

Malcolm Jackson arrived at the Sonic Security Systems building less than ten minutes later. He was ushered to a conference room on the ground floor. Jason walked in before Malcolm had sat down.

"Jason Spencer?" Jackson asked.

"Yes, and you are?" Jason asked, rubbing his hands and then wiping them on his trousers.

"Detective Jackson with the Durham Police Department," Jackson said with a faint smile. "Please have a seat. You're not in trouble or anything; I just have a few questions."

Jason sat down opposite the detective. "Personal or business."

"I think personal, but we'll see where this goes," Jackson said as he retrieved a small notepad from his jacket pocket.

"OK, that's strange, but go ahead; I hope you don't bring bad news or something."

"I don't think so," the detective said. "When was the last time you spoke with your parents?"

"Did something happen to them?" Jason said, sitting up straight, one hand over his heart.

"Well, their neighbors are a bit concerned because they left town, and we can't locate them."

"You mean the neighbors in Durham?"

"Yes."

Jason seemed to relax and sat back in his chair. "Well, that's an easy one. They have another home in Florida. I'm sure you can find them there if you want to talk with them. I have their number."

"Are you aware they sold their house in Florida last week?"

"What? No. Are you sure?" Jason said, appearing genuinely surprised.

"We have confirmation from a real estate agent there."

Jason looked around the room and at the ceiling, perhaps trying to wrap his head around this new information. "I don't know what to say. They loved that place in The Villages. I don't get it."

"I reckon they didn't share any plans with you then?"

"No, detective. I had no clue."

"And did they share where they were going?"

"If they are no longer in Florida, they should be in Durham," Jason said, slowing down when he spoke those last words. "But, as you said, they're not there."

"Now, I don't want you to panic unnecessarily, but they did run into a neighbor a few days ago at RDU Airport. Your father claimed that they were flying to Florida. Would they vacation there?"

"Why would they do that? They've seen everything in the state. I still don't get why they've sold the house."

"We may get an answer if we could get in touch with them...."

"So, you've tried to call them?"

"Their concerned neighbors have."

"I haven't talked with them in a week, but if their phone is on and Dad has WiFi or a cell signal, I can find out where they are. Do you want me to do that?"

"I believe that should indeed be our next step."

"Wait, you haven't told me why you want to talk with them. Are they in trouble for something?"

"Do you think they are?" Jackson asked.

Jason hesitated. "My parents are good people, detective. They've been really helpful to my family. They drive up whenever they can and stay for a few weeks. Then it's back down to Florida because they're involved in so many things there, and they miss their friends and neighbors."

"I get that, Jason, but that appears to be over now that they only have the home in Durham. In a way, it's tough to have to commute between two homes, 600 miles apart," Jackson said after scribbling in his notepad."

"But why is that of interest to you, detective?"

"As I said, their neighbors are alarmed that your parents are missing. I'm simply following up. So, let's focus on that now."

"I still don't get why those neighbors want to know where my parents are. I'm sure there's a good explanation," Jason said, not ready to help out by finding where they were.

"There's a bit more than that," Jackson admitted, dropping his notepad on the table. "You see, we have reliable information that they may have been contacted by people who take advantage of senior citizens, and...."

"You mean they may have been scammed?" Jason interrupted.

"Something like that. I was told they drove up often because your business here is in financial trouble, and they gave you money to help out."

"What the hell? That's not the case at all. The company is doing very well, as a matter of fact. Look around," Jason said, waving his arm around the conference. "We are growing daily in revenues and employees. Who told you that?"

"That's what your parents told their Durham neighbors. This was why they came up so often to give you money," Jackson answered, putting his hands together in praying mode. He seemed ready to get some valuable information.

Jason laughed. "That's my parents, alright," he said. "They'd never admit that something so bad couldn't be solved by money. I think they took that plausible explanation, and I get that. The truth is that there's a real issue which, yes, requires a lot of money, but it is not the business."

"And the problem is?"

Jason sat back and took a deep breath. Jackson noticed sudden shiny moisture in the young man's eyes. He briefly expected him to cry, but Jason swallowed hard and leaned forward.

"My parents didn't want to share that our daughter, Ellie, is, or has been, seriously ill. She was diagnosed three years ago with a rare form of dystrophy leukemia. She's on the mend, but it has cost us a lot because our insurance only covered eighty percent of all costs. My parents helped out with the remaining bills."

"I'm sorry to hear about your child, Jason," Jackson said, continuing to take notes. "I understand your parents didn't want to share that but were glad to help financially."

"Thank you. You see, that's why they come up so often. They want to be with Ellie as much as possible. She's their only grandchild."

"And it must feel good that they can help out financially."

"Of course. Do you have any idea how much a single chemo session costs? All the maintenance drugs? My wife Erin is working as much as possible, but she's the primary caregiver, detective," Jason explained. "Every month, we're about 10K short, which has been going on for a few years."

"I'm glad you said your daughter's getting better, right?"

"Yes. She's now on a bi-monthly Immuno treatment which we can afford."

"This would explain that your parents no longer need to help out, right?"

"True. I think they've depleted their savings because they'd contributed a ton of money. I realize now that this is why they sold their home in The Villages. It makes sense that they choose to keep the house in Durham as they want to be close to Ellie."

"That sounds plausible," Jackson agreed. "The issue remains that they told their neighbor they were going to Florida." He paused and flipped a few pages back in his notepad. "There's a letter from a real estate agent waiting for them to be signed urgently. This is concerning the house they sold. I believe not signing it is holding up the closing. So, I wanted to return to my initial question to find out where your parents are."

"I understand," Jason said. He picked up his phone. "What kind of detective are you anyway?" Jason casually asked while pushing a few buttons.

"I handle narcotics and illegal drug trafficking in the department."

Jason held off tapping his phone and looked up, wide-eyed and his lower jaw dropping. "What? Drugs? That's what you think my parents are involved in?"

"I have no proof of that. I was just called in because your parents made a lot of trips from Florida to North Carolina."

"And? What does that mean?"

"It simply means someone may have given them something to bring up North. They may not even know what it was. There's no case, Jason. I just want to talk to them to let them know about the letter and perhaps give some answers. Those might dispel any suspicion, you see."

"Ok then," Jason said and returned his attention to his phone. "Let me see if I can locate them."

He tapped a few more times and waited. As his phone lay flat on the table, Jackson could clearly see the upside-down map with the blue dot. They both saw the island of St. Maarten in the Caribbean.

"On vacation after all," the detective said.

"That's a first," Jason said, looking up. "They never mentioned they were going anywhere."

"Can you call them, please?"

Jason nodded and dialed. His dad picked up. "Hey, Dad. I can't believe you guys are in St. Maarten. I just tracked you. What's going on?"

Jackson didn't hear the reply and waited patiently while Jason nodded and few times. "So, you're staying a whole month?" The answer seemed to be a long one. "Just wanted you and Mom to know there's a letter from the real estate agent in Florida. I can't believe you sold the house."

Jason waited for his dad to end his explanation. "So, okay, I'll sign that for you as I have a power of attorney. Great, I'll take care of that. Say hi to Mom and call me next week." He listened. "Dad, before you hang up, I have a question. Did anyone lately give you a package to bring up north here?"

The question wasn't answered as the connection was lost.

Chapter 21

Sam

Everyone has weaknesses and desires. For the users who eventually bought the goods Sam Vanderlaan had shipped from Florida to New York, it was the high they felt when they first started using. Later, it was relief from the incredible pain they felt when their supply was somehow cut off. For the Spencers, it was the comfortable payment of bills, paid for by the easy cash they received for transporting packages. This was as easy as traveling between their home in The Villages and the one in the Carolina Arbors. The prospect of easy money soon morphed into the need for more money for their granddaughter's treatment until the money became an all-consuming dragon they couldn't get off their backs.

Sam had grown up in a conservative middle-class family with a solid Dutch heritage. They were not poor but never had a luxurious lifestyle either. After high school, he began working for an insurance agency in Scranton near his hometown.

He had a taste for nice clothes, pretty girls, fast cars and expensive toys. *I'll never get what I want working in an insurance office,* he had thought. Then one day, he was called into the boss's office at the headquarters in New York. "You know, Sammy, we sell all kinds of insurance here," his boss, Mr. Bonelli, said. "You work a little more, take on a little more responsibility, and pretty soon, you don't have to wear a suit from J.C. Penny. Maybe Men's Warehouse suits look nicer on you. They carry Calvin Klein." That's when Sam started doing "errands." He sorely wanted the clothes and the women and the cars. He didn't look too hard at the errands he was asked to do. Maybe smash up a magazine stand owner's face, break a tailor's sewing arm, burn down a little deli? It was just business. After all, they shouldn't have taken out loans if they couldn't make the payments.

Soon, Sam has a rap sheet a mile long and several years on the State's nickel to his credit. It gave him enough to give him street cred with the higher-ups in the city's criminal organizations. After his last year inside, the Boss figured he was too well known on the East Coast to keep working in Philadelphia. He was sent to North Carolina to handle "shipping" for the organization. "Keep your nose clean down there, Sammy. We want a steady flow of merchandise and no foul-ups." A little later, the Boss and a few of his lieutenants were arrested for the murder of Sloppy Joe. Sam had a new boss he called Mr. Big.

Sam was set up in a nice condo near Raleigh and one in Ocala. He began prospecting for mules in Florida with connections in North Carolina and vice versa. He participated in events where insurance companies were invited to give their spiel to retirement communities. He worked his angle at recreation centers every few months as an insurance salesman with New York offices. He treated people to big plates of free food and tons of pens. He figured those were things that attracted retirees. Once a couple signed up to talk insurance, he judged to see if they were perfect to become well-paid couriers to ferry innocent-looking packages along I-95. For now, he was all set and spent most of his time in North Carolina, overseeing the drops.

To be sure, Sam Vanderlaan had never killed anyone. That isn't to say that people who crossed him didn't end up dead. He was just careful not to be personally involved in their deaths. Sam knew that when you controlled the supply of a substance so wanted that desperate people would kill for, you too could determine people who needed killing. That's why Joe Malinski was in big trouble, but the man didn't know it yet.

Sam always wondered why people had to involve themselves in situations that were not really any of their business. So the Spencers were picking up a little extra cash running some juice up north. They might as well be driving for Amazon or FedEx. He always referred to the street name 'juice' for laced opioids. His day would turn out great whenever he took a pill in the morning before breakfast. He figured people who needed medicine were getting it any way they could. At least some stuck-up doctor in a fancy office wasn't paying off his medical school student loans by supplying drugs to desperate users he had probably gotten addicted. What the hell was the difference? No one was getting hurt; even drug dealers had quality control.

None of this usually occupied Sam's mind, but Mr. Big in Flatbush did. Mr. Big concerned him a lot. He'd never met the man himself. Their business was always conducted through cut-offs. Third-party punks delivered messages, packages, and cash and did what they were told when and how. Sam knew that if they were told to break both of the courier's arms or legs, they'd think no more of that than delivering a thick envelope filled with cash at some shady location.

With a street value of over 500K per drop, protecting the merchandise from other gangs or onlookers was important. He often checked up on the guys who handled business at the drop zones. He took care not to be spotted during the transactions. Although he sometimes was needed in Ocala, he primarily operated in Durham. Sometimes he'd seen a car parked near the drop zone, but he usually didn't treat that as a problem if there was no movement. After the Spencers' last drop, he stayed for a while. He didn't notice anything out of the ordinary. A few days later, another drop by another mule, he stayed out of sight for about ten minutes after the business was concluded. To his surprise, someone drove up, clearly scouting the parking lot. That guy was careless, and when he dove into the trash bin, Sam sat up straight. A few days earlier, he'd seen Fabio Spencer discard his boxes. The guy snooping around was clearly on a mission, taking out the boxes and snapping pictures. That evening, Sam followed the nosy guy to his home.

The first thing to do was learn more about this "Mr. Stick-His-Nose-in-Someone-Else's-Business." The next day, Sam found the name of Joe Malinski associated with the address. After a quick call to Mr. Big, he decided to check out this Joe. He'd already seen him talk excitedly to a neighbor when he got home. Realizing that this Joe was a neighbor of the Spencers was troubling, to say the least. Sam soon found out that Joe was an ex-detective with Big Apple ties. To Sam, a giant red flag was waving at hurricane strength. This Joe character likely was on to them. Undoubtedly, he knew the Spencers well, and he might be the guy who would confront the Spencers about what he may have discovered. Definitely a problem because the Spencers, until now, had no issues or confrontations during their runs or drops. He figured that Joe wasn't talking to anyone else yet, primarily because, as an old detective, he'd want all the facts and details before contacting the local fuzz.

Sam had one job to do, as Mr. Big's boys were fond of repeatedly telling him. Even though he never handled packages himself, he knew they either contained drugs or cash. No one could prove that knowledge, so that no one could testify in court. His pay was good. There wasn't much work involved, but the worst part of the deal was keeping an eye on the mules. He liked naive old couples who had gotten too deep into their new retirement situation. That ideal runner fit the Spencers to a T.

The Spencers had indeed been perfect finds for him. They were a lovely couple who effortlessly made the trips back and forth even in their late sixties. He thought it was funny that he had recruited them in a restaurant called NYPD Pizzeria on Wedgewood in Ocala. Two mules who liked to hang around the NYPD. That was a laugh. The State Troopers would never pay any attention to two silver-haired seniors driving through their state with a stack of boxes in the trunk, some disguised as gift-wrapped presents, if they ever even looked back there.

There had been a problem when Fabio figured out the contents of what they were delivering. Still, a warning of outing them and disclosing unknown sources of their tax-free cash to the IRS office in Florida or North Carolina had quieted his objections. They had a job they couldn't quit, and they knew it.

Everything had been perfect until this Malinski character butted in.

Present Times

Chapter 22

July 4th

Lydia counted the minutes until the time Ramón had told her they were to leave. Travis Vinder's home party was attended by the Durham Police Department colleagues and neighbors in the active retirement community. She had made up her mind: having conversations with cops about burgers and hotdogs was not a fave. Neither were the old geezers who insisted she participate in every game like bocce ball, horseshoes and cornhole. Was it a coincidence that they were all playing games which frankly didn't serve her well, considering her short skirt? Upon arriving at the party, she immediately realized that perhaps her outfit should have been a bit more modest. Ramón had liked her white blouse tied under her breasts, exposing her belly button just above her red skirt. A blue cap with the gothic letter D for Duke didn't prove a good choice when some guests, obviously UNC fans, constantly commented on it. It would have been different if she'd attended the school. Still, a nursing degree from a community college in Florida was as far as she'd gotten. Lydia smiled, thinking she might be called upon if someone at the party took a fall or something. That would get her some respect. She'd returned the hat to the car and combed her blond hair. While getting a glass of water, she realized it would've been wise to listen more closely to Ramón when he had told her about the party and who'd be there. She also should have asked what kind of games they'd be playing. Lesson learned, she figured.

She was approached by a younger fellow at the drinks table, definitely not a neighbor. "Hi," he smiled, showing his white teeth contrasting nicely against his dark skin. "Hi, who are you?" Lydia asked as she picked up her glass.

"You here with Ramón Acosta, right?" he asked.

"Yes," she replied and turned as if reminded to look for her boyfriend.

"I'm Frankie," he said, sticking out his hand. Lydia shook it, and he continued. "Ramón's a great guy. You must be proud of him for passing that detective's exam."

"Oh, he was determined to finish with success. He had a great coach in Travis for the past two years. So, you're with the department as well?"

"Yes, downtown Durham is my beat. There's more action there in one day than you'd see in this neighborhood in a year."

"Hah, unless you want to arrest some of these neighbors here for ogling young women," Lydia laughed. "Anyway, nice meeting you. I've got to find Ramón."

"Same here," Frankie said and poured another beer into his cup. As Lydia wandered off into the back yard, his eyes followed her.

Lydia walked through the house to the front and took the opportunity to stop by the bathroom. As soon as she locked the door, the party noise seriously dulled. It was easy to pick up on a conversation in an adjoining room. At first, she wasn't sure who was speaking as the voices seemed subdued, but soon she could make out Travis. Judging by the sudden raising of voices and the subject, she concluded that he was arguing with his wife. "If you believe that, why did you bother coming back? You should've stayed in Philadelphia," Travis shouted. "I would've if I knew you were having it on with her while I was taking care of my dad," she heard Maureen yell.

A door slammed, and Lydia backed off the wall she'd put her ear to. She flushed and walked out, heading straight back to the back of the house, not looking to see whether it was Travis or Maureen who had left that room. Once outside, she saw Ramón.

"Ah, there you are," he smiled, putting his arm around her waist. "I heard you met Frankie."

"Yes, I did. Were you two partners on the force?"

"We never teamed up, but we did share a class at Wake Tech. He also wants to be a detective and is going through the requirements. He's got a ways to go, though."

"I see. So, are we still planning on getting out of here around seven?"

"Yes, we have to wait until dessert. I think Travis has a little speech in mind. It looks like you've had it with playing games and schmoozing with the neighbors."

"Are you kidding? I didn't do the schmoozing. I was the trophy everyone wanted on their team," Lydia laughed. "Seriously though, can't we get away for a while?"

"Sure. Do you want to go for a walk in the neighborhood? We'll make sure we're back well before seven. I'll tell Travis."

"Great. No more yard games. I'm over it."

"I get it. Wait here; I'll be back in a minute."

Lydia turned and stared directly at Frankie, standing just two feet away. "Oh, you again," she said, regretting how it sounded. "I mean, nice to see you again."

"I was actually going to speak to Ramón, but I didn't want to interrupt the two of you. Then he just left," Frankie smiled.

"Oh, I'm sorry," Lydia said. "He'll be back in a minute."

"It's not urgent anyway," Frankie said, taking a sip of his beer. "You guys hanging here the whole evening?"

"We don't plan on it. We're going for a short walk, and then we're leaving after dessert. More hotdogs and burgers at Ramón's mother's place, followed by fireworks."

"Sounds exciting. Anyway, nice meeting you," Frankie said. "I think I'm going to beat someone at cornhole."

Lydia turned back, and this time Ramón stood in front of her, and he grabbed her hand. "Let's go; Travis told me where we can go."

***

The humid and hot Carolina air made way for a much cooler version with plenty of shade once Ramón and Lydia left the sidewalk and entered a wooded area. A slight breeze made the oppressive air more palpable. The birds were stealthily hiding on shaded branches as it was quiet and calm around them. Lydia took a deep breath. "Ah, away from all the people. This greenway is awesome."

"Yeah, stepping away for a short while feels good."

"If anything, it keeps you away from another beer," Lydia laughed.

"Max two, considering we have a long drive to my Mom's house."

"True," Lydia said and walked on quietly.

A few residents walked by in the opposite direction. Everyone said hello or nodded. Dogs proceeded owners who carried green plastic bags.

"Friendly neighborhood," Ramón remarked.

"I can't believe you said that so casually," Lydia objected. "Didn't you tell me there were three murders here in the past few years?"

"I did, but only one case had this neighborhood involved. I talked to some fellows at the picnic, and you won't believe some things are happening here. Sometimes I think that all the people here reflect the country's state. Very divisive."

"Oh, like what?"

"Apparently, there's a discussion about whether people should be allowed to park one or two cars in their driveway."

"You're kidding."

"No, and some of their arguments are ridiculous and their discussions heated. We had to step in and separate two guys. Travis asked them to go home."

"So, all's not perfect in paradise?"

"Well, judging Travis's comments, living here is great. He figured there always would be some people who'd buck the norm and some who abhor any change. Such is life."

"Yeah, but what gives with the cars? What difference does it make?"

"All I gathered is that it's a visual and for others a functional issue."

"Don't they have guidelines for things like that?"

"I'm sure they have HOA rules and such."

"Crazy," Lydia said, looking at the big building to her right. 'Hey, I wonder what that is? Can we take this path?"

"That's the clubhouse," Ramón said. "Nice place. I've been there several times. Unfortunately, that's where that last murder took place."

"I don't want to go in; I just want to walk by it," Lydia said.

They took the blacktopped path and walked past the clubhouse. Lydia noticed that the wooden bridges were numbered. "How many bridges are there?"

Ramón briefly raised his shoulders. "Don't know. I've only been on a few paths here and there while on another case." He paused. "So, Travis told me we can continue across the main road here and take that path. We can return to his house by following it to the left."

"Good. I hate to get lost," Lydia smiled and squeezed his hand. "I'm counting on you to keep me safe."

"You're in good hands," Ramón squeezed back lightly.

After a brief moment of silence, they heard the noise of people. "Sounds like they're having a party at the pool."

"There's a pool? I wish I knew; we might have taken a swim to cool off."

"As a matter of fact, I asked Travis. He said that guests were not allowed on holidays."

"What? That's when people have company, and what a better place to go to on a hot day like today."

"Travis said that their HOA board is constantly subject to criticism. It's like a paradise of lost opportunities in the neighborhood."

Lydia laughed. "I'm sure things will settle. I mean, these people are retired and all."

"Maybe. People are rightly pissed off when stupid rules interfere with their lifestyle."

The next bridge they crossed appeared higher off the ground underneath as their steps sounded like they walked over a hollow chamber. Lydia looked at the small brook that flowed underneath to her left. She noticed a patch of blackberry bushes that still had some fruit and couldn't resist. "I love those," she said and worked her way down on the other side of the bridge toward the water. Ramón stayed on the bridge, leaning over. "Be careful of the troll living there!" he said.

Lydia humored him. "Oh yeah? What does he look like?"

"Short and stocky with big teeth, ready to take a yummy bite out of your leg."

Lydia picked a few berries, blew on them as there were covered with something and then popped them in her mouth. "Yeah, yeah. No troll here. You wouldn't come and rescue me. I know you're afraid of trolls. That's why you're not coming down here."

"Hey, I need to stay here in case someone sends his dog down there."

Lydia had moved on, now partly under the bridge.

"Seen that troll yet?" Ramón called down. The answer wasn't what he expected. Lydia screamed at the top of her lungs.

"Ramón, someone is down here. Oh my God!" she said as she backed away and ran back to the head of the bridge.

"What are you talking about?" Ramón asked, running up to her.

"I think someone is lying down there," Lydia said, shaking and hugging herself.

Ramón grabbed her gently by the shoulders. "Okay, rest here against the side of the bridge," he said. I'll be back in a sec." Lydia nodded and closed her eyes while Ramón ran to the spot where Lydia disappeared under the bridge. He carefully stepped in her footsteps to avoid further disturbing the area. He quickly realized this might be a possible crime scene as he stared at a motionless body. It appeared to be a man wearing white socks, blue shorts and a red polo. The back of his head showed a big gaping wound, similar to an injury caused by a gun fired at close range. Ramón briefly looked around the area and retreated carefully. He walked back onto the bridge and hugged his girlfriend. "I think we can forget about the dessert. I have to call this in."

Lydia nodded and stared into the woods. She'd never seen a dead person, and this was seriously off the charts. How did Ramón deal with all of this? She grabbed the railing tight and thought of how her life would be living with a detective. From what she heard a bit earlier, Travis's marriage didn't exactly set an example. No idea what happened there, but something wasn't right. She felt confused and turned back toward Ramón, who was on the phone. She listened in.

"Are you calling the forensics team?" he asked and nodded when Travis had confirmed. "Okay, we'll wait for you here."

***

Travis arrived well before the coroner and the Durham Forensics team got there. Lydia saw him walking between two police cars parked near the path entrance. Still in shorts, he approached the bridge. Ramón had just sent a few walkers away.

"This way," Ramón motioned to Travis. They walked to the end of the bridge and followed the path Lydia had taken first. Travis looked for footprints and carefully stepped closer to the body while putting on latex gloves.

"Can you take a few pictures? I'm not going to turn the body, just the head, but I want to ensure we record how the body was placed."

Travis stepped back briefly to give Ramón a clear view. He squatted down and slowly turned the bloody head until he could see most of the face. His lower jaw dropped instantly and froze. Someone had killed New York's ex-detective, Joe Malinski.

Chapter 23

The Bridge

Detective Vinder remembered his first visit to Joe Malinski's home at the Arbors. He'd been a healthy man, ran at least five miles a day and didn't look a day over sixty. He was seventy-three. As a retired NYPD detective assigned to the Street Crimes Unit until the late eighties, he'd helped solve the murder at Piedmont Hall. Joe knew the lay of the land regarding gangs and the mafia. That case had a lot to do with both. Travis recalled that Joe divulged that he'd had a series of transient ischemic attacks or mini-strokes. Nevertheless, he had pointed the team in the right direction since that murder was solved with information from characters who'd lived in his old beat. The situation here may have something to do with the closed case.

"What are you contemplating?" Ramón asked.

Travis got up. "I was just thinking about meeting this man last year. He was instrumental in getting me to the real identity of the murder victim."

"Right, I do remember that. So, do you think this has something to do with that case? That's mafia! A case of vengeance?"

"Not sure, Ramón. Let's discuss it away from here."

The forensic unit had stepped in and was making its first assessments. Away from the bridge, Travis continued.

"All the guys in that Mafia line of command are currently in jail," he said, rubbing his forehead. He slowly turned around and stared at nothing particular in the woods.

"From what I've learned, this is a classic execution. Gunshot to the back of the head."

"That's what I'm struggling with. It appears indeed to have been an execution, but I can't quite connect this to the other case."

"Maybe forensics will get us some clues."

"There's something that bothers me, though," Travis said.

"What?"

"Joe called me a while back about a possible drug smuggling case in this neighborhood. He sent me a bunch of pictures of what looked like a dropping point in Durham. There were several shots of boxes with names and addresses on them. I turned it all over to Detective Jackson since he deals with narcotics cases. Never heard back from him."

"That indeed could be a better connection to this crime than the old case," Ramón mused.

Travis looked back at the taped-off area where men dressed in white Tyvek's outfits, including hoods, boots, and gloves, were busy scouring the area under the bridge. "I know Joe lived alone, but he's got to have family in New York. Get the paperwork going so you can go through his house. I'm sure you'll turn up some information, detective," Travis said as he gently slapped Ramón on the shoulder.

Ramón walked over to Lydia, sitting on a grassy slope away from the scene. She had crossed her arms and rested them on her knees tucked up toward her chest. Her head, partly propped on her arms, was mostly covered by her hair draped over her hands. She popped her head up when she heard Ramón call her name. "Are you done?"

"Let's go," Ramón said with a wry smile, betraying the seriousness of the situation that would indeed require his attention. He helped Lydia to her feet, and they walked past the bridge to return to Travis' home.

"I'd love to go to my parent's home with you, but I've got some things to do given the situation here."

"How am I going to get to Siler City, Ramón? Remember, you picked me up."

"Use my car. I'm off tomorrow, and we can meet up then. I'm sorry this party's a bust."

"I gather we only missed dessert and a speech," Lydia reminded him.

"Right. No big deal. I understand. Are you okay with driving home?"

"Sure. Don't worry. I'll hold the fireworks for you. Maybe we can see some tomorrow where they're having July 5th celebrations."

"Yeah, right," Ramón said. "Maybe I can get a squad car and come over later when I'm done with everything."

"What is it that you have to do?"

"Tracking down the victim's family and letting them know what happened. I may have to go there depending on where they live. They may be out of state or far away. Then I'd involve another police department to deliver the message personally."

"Sounds like the ugly side of a murder case," Lydia offered as she put her hand on his arm.

They crossed the street. "Actually, nothing is ever pretty in a homicide case."

"So why do you want to do it?"

"I guess it's the satisfaction of solving the case and apprehending the killer or killers. It's a good feeling knowing that those people can no longer hurt anyone else."

"Did you ever consider investigating white-collar crime, like financial crooks or theft?" Ramón didn't answer but smiled, briefly cocking his head. They didn't talk until reaching Travis' house a half-minute later, where the party was still going strong. Nobody seemed to miss the host, and Maureen had taken charge of dessert and drinks.

He then answered Lydia. "I did. And rest assured, there're times that there're no homicide cases, old or new, and we assist other detectives. So, yes, I do that, but now that I'm in this department, I want to do the best I can."

"I get it," Lydia said. "I'm glad you're dedicated to your new job, though I'm struggling with the hours, and I'm not sure I can handle that in a relationship."

She put both hands on Ramón's shoulders. "Do you know what I mean?"

Ramón nodded and looked her straight in the eyes. "I do. I know you're concerned. Do you know what? I just thought of something. Perhaps I only need to be here an hour or so. Do you want to stick around? I need to make some calls and then go to that Mr. Malinski's house."

"And then what?" Lydia asked.

"If I find what I'm looking for, I either need to contact someone or drive to a relative's home."

"You don't even know where you'd have to go...."

"As I said, I can have another department take care of it if it's too far. Don't worry, we may have to skip my mom's dinner, but we'll be at your home before the fireworks start. I promise."

Lydia slanted her head slightly and narrowed her eyes. "Hmm," she said briefly and stepped toward Ramón's car.

"So you're in?" he called after her.

"Let's go," she said as she opened the passenger door. Ten seconds later, Ramón was on the phone with the precinct.

***

Travis had returned to a cleared spot under the bridge. Stephan, the chief forensic specialist, told him the area had been checked, and his team combed through other places.

"When will you be able to move the body?" Travis asked after a while.

"We'll be another ten minutes, detective," Stephan said.

Travis nodded and retrieved his phone, looking up Joe Malinski's phone number and address. He dialed the number. There was no answer, and after four rings, the connection ended in his voice mail. The phone didn't ring nearby either. He called the station, and it seemed to ring forever. The operator he finally talked with connected him to the warrants desk. He understood the staffing issue on a holiday but expected a faster response.

"Hey, happy fourth," he said. "Listen, detective Acosta will be calling in soon. He needs to go into the house of a murder victim, and I believe that person lived alone. Can you help him out?"

After receiving an affirmative answer, he put his phone away and waited until the white suits were done. He saw two men looking in the small river and alongside the overgrown banks. One had a metal detector but kept shaking his head.

Travis knew that a professional killer wouldn't just ditch the gun. So, there was nothing to trace, and unless they found an empty shell, it would be tough to match all this to another case. That is, if the weapon was used there, of course. He noticed that Stephan and an assistant were turning over the body. He immediately saw a deep imprint of the victim's knees in the soft soil in front of the small creek. It proved what he had already feared: Joe was told to sit on his knees and was then executed. The bullet had gone through, and the gaping exit wound on the forehead indicated that it was most likely a .45 that did the damage. The forensics measured the approximate angle and projected a red beam from where the head might have been to the small area on the other side of the stream. If that was the path the bullet followed, they might be in luck finding the slug. Stephan called over the assistant with the detector.

The detective nodded and stepped in closer to look at the body. It took only two minutes to retrieve the remnant of what indeed appeared to be a .45 caliber bullet. Another assistant bagged the evidence and held it up for Travis to see.

"Any idea about the time of death?"

"Two hours ago, maybe three," Stephan said. "We'll know more once we take the body in."

"So, he was killed here, right?" Travis asked the obvious.

"It appears so. I think the vic was walking on the path and dragged down here. He has no ID or keys on him."

"Can you tell if a silencer was used? I know this isn't near any house, but I guess people would still hear a gunshot from this greenway."

"I can't tell at this point. Someone is bound to have heard it. I don't think we have a gun alert detector nearby, so it may not appear on our system. Triangulation would be hard to do in this case. Without that, we'll let the coroner figure out the time of death."

"So, I guess we'll canvas the houses within a quarter-mile from this spot."

"You've got your work cut out, detective."

"I know," Travis sighed. "Another Carolina Arbors Murder."

Chapter 24

Charlotte

Bad things just keep happening, Charlotte mused as she walked toward her morning water aerobics class. Something evil had entered the Arbors, but she didn't know exactly what it was. Things just felt wrong. Even short walks felt creepy, and Charlotte sensed that she wasn't the only one who felt that way. Another murder! The fourth one in as many years.

This time it was that sweet man, Joe Malinski. He had been such a nice man, a retired detective, active in community projects, always with a friendly smile and an eagerness to chat with his neighbors. Charlotte, with her Southern roots, appreciated that. Although retirement community members were becoming more social, some neighbors remained stiff and aloof. Some would fail to respond to a polite wave or even a warm hello. Joe wasn't that way at all.

Charlotte thought about her last few conversations with Joe and realized that he had also noticed something wrong. How long ago had that been? They had bumped into each other on the way out of the Piedmont Hall lecture on illegal drug use and distribution routes. At that time, Joe shared information he recalled from his old job about the I-95 and I85 routes that had been the primary highways used by couriers for decades. He mentioned how he wondered about the overuse of drugs in our community and mules living among us.

He also suggested that she keep her eyes open because he knew her keen observation skills had been crucial in assisting the police. When her neighbor Jeanne appeared, Charlotte told Joe a quick goodbye, and the two women headed for their street. Charlotte remarked to Jeanne that the warm darkness didn't feel as safe as before the lecture. Still, she kept the conversation with Joe to herself, resolving to see if she could satisfactorily arrange his musings and the things she heard at the talk in her mind.

***

Several days later, Charlotte and Jeanne ran into Joe and Mary while walking on one of the trails. She asked Joe whether he had learned more about the smuggling routes when a quick sharp glance and a slight headshake had silenced her. But as Jeanne and Mary discussed the previous night's Bunco and the holiday plans for the approaching Fourth of July, Joe had pulled her aside. He whispered that he didn't want to discuss smuggling drugs in front of others. A few minutes later, they all moved on. She was a bit puzzled why Joe acted like that. Was he afraid to talk about smugglers? She had wanted to mention that she'd occasionally seen a particular car parked close to his house. A man was always sitting in the driver's seat, often with open windows. She was sure that the stranger kept an eye on Joe's house. Then, after their chance encounter, she hadn't seen that car again, and she didn't feel like bringing it up with Joe until the day before Independence Day when the car was back.

That morning, she purposely took a longer route passing by Joe's house. Perhaps he was sitting on his porch or was tidying his yard. Maybe she'd mention that car. However, as she neared his house, there was no sign of Joe. She did see that large black Yukon Denali parked near his home again. She decided to walk up to the car. All the windows were closed, and she noticed they were all darkly tinted. Shifting reflections in the glass seemed to indicate movement in the vehicle. She had dubbed the man inside a spy before. Was he back? And was he spying? Or was he stalking one of the neighbors, Mary? Charlotte momentarily thought of tapping on the window to get the attention of the person inside. After all, the car was parked on the wrong side of the street. The HOA "parking police" might be especially vigilant on a holiday with numerous guests and visitors. It might be nice of her to inform the spy, she chuckled.

As she continued to look, she altered her mind. Was it her imagination, or did the car have a vaguely sinister appearance? She almost shuddered as she continued past but turned to take another look. The license plate read *You've Got a Friend in Pennsylvania*. Definitely an out-of-town vehicle. She quickly committed the plate number to memory and then noticed a change in the shadows in the back window. Had someone turned to look at her? Did he realize that she'd been looking at his plate numbers? Cold chills crept up her spine as she moved on down the sidewalk. It was hard to maintain the same pace when she wanted to run. Don't be silly, Charlotte, she chided herself. That was then.

On the morning of July 4th Charlotte started her morning walk a little early. She needed to prepare her famous/infamous Mississippi Mud cake for her block party, but without the bourbon whipped cream. Her neighbors would pretend to worry about the cake being laced with a drug and do a lot of sniffing and eye-rolling. Then they'd have a hearty laugh and eat huge portions. They were all in on the joke. Honestly, she couldn't believe how much trouble those few drops of a precious Mexican sedative had caused her.

Later that day, the laughter of community block parties and other gatherings had been snuffed out by the rapidly spreading news that Joe Malinsky's body had been discovered under a bridge on one of the trails.

Charlotte and the other neighbors were rapid with their goodbyes, their faces horrified. She gathered her things, did her share of the clean-up, and silently made her way home like the others on the block. As soon as she closed her door, she stretched out face down on her bed and indulged in a good cry.

Later that evening, the nagging thought that she needed to share that car information with the police continued to torment her. Charlotte knew her information was important, but she hated to contact Vinder. He always made her feel like a small, silly old woman. Rationally she knew that he resented her because his rush to judgment in the mud cake crime had embarrassed him. However, he still hadn't warmed to her despite the valuable information she had supplied in the other Arbor murder cases. Now Ramón Acosta was another person entirely. That handsome young man always greeted her with a friendly smile and sometimes a casual wink if no one was looking. It made her feel that they shared a private joke, and really, they did. Ramón instinctively knew how Vinder felt about her; these small signals were his way of letting her know he didn't share those feelings.

What to do, and how long should she wait? She couldn't call Ramón because that would be going over Vinder's head, a thing that was always actively frowned upon. Besides, Ramón did not live in the Arbors, and Vinder did. Anonymity was impossible because it would undermine credibility. Ah, she had a brilliant thought! She could tell her friend, Barbara, about the vehicle she'd seen. She's seen her and Vinder talk once at the clubhouse, and they appeared to be friends. Should she call tonight or wait until tomorrow morning?

Chapter 25

Family

The coroner showed up at the start of the greenway off Del Webb Arbors Drive as Travis headed back home. One side of the road was completely blocked off. A firetruck, an ambulance, and four police cars had kept their lights flashing. It looked like an early preview of many fireworks to come that evening. He told two officers to start canvassing the streets running parallel to the path. After making sure they'd call him with the address of people who heard something and when, he headed for his house.

The party was still on, and most officers from his department were in on what had transpired. As he walked into his back yard, all the guests walked up to him. He briefed them with short statements of fact, omitting the victim's name, how he was killed, and where it took place. Of course, questions zeroed in on this, but he kept telling them that's all he could confirm for now. He did add that the police were looking for residents who might have heard a gunshot.

He grabbed a water bottle and noticed that neighbors were suddenly leaving. Slowly the colleagues peeled away too after saying goodbye to Maureen and Travis. He didn't feel like cleaning up and used the new case as an excuse to leave.

"Figures that you leave me with all this to clean up," Maureen said sharply.

"Don't wait up for me. It may be late. We'll talk tomorrow."

Maureen didn't respond as she opened a black garbage bag. Travis went inside, changed his clothes and took off. His first stop was at the crime scene.

***

It took over an hour for the warrant to be issued. Once Ramón got the call and having already established that nobody was at the home of Mr. Malinski, he opened the garage door via the side panel. A neighbor had shared the code and was satisfied that everything was being done according to the book. Lydia stayed in the car and was on her phone with her mother.

The neighbor also volunteered that Joe's family lived in New Jersey and Winston-Salem. That was a start. He squirmed his hands into the blue latex gloves.

From the garage, the door to the house was unlocked. Ramón put his hands on his hips and looked around the living room and kitchen. He quickly spotted a picture of small children and a larger family picture that stood nicely framed next to the TV. In it, Joe stood behind four adults. In front of them, he counted five children. There were three men and a woman. She had blond hair, and three girls' hair matched the color. The two boys were very young, maybe three and six years old. Everyone smiled. Ramón's best guess was that he looked at the patriarch and two couples with their children. The picture was taken at Disney.

He opened a few drawers and found paperwork relating to the house, a checkbook, pencils and post-it notes. No address book. He texted Travis. Ten seconds later, a phone rang in the house. He spotted it in the bedroom on a small dresser opposite the bed. He pressed the green button. "Got it."

"Good, if it doesn't lock on you when you hang up. If it does, you'll need to find addresses differently."

"He's got two sons, I believe. One may have adopted two boys; the other has three daughters. I already know their state locations, but I have no address or number."

"Ask the neighbors. If you find an address, call it in."

"Right. Are you back at the bridge?"

"Finishing up here, waiting for the result of a neighborhood canvass. Someone may have heard a shot fired."

"Unless a silencer was used."

"It's possible. Are you going to inform the family?"

"Most likely not, unless you want me to drive to Winston-Salem."

"No, the local force will take care of that. Keep me posted on what you find, and we'll talk tomorrow."

Ramón hung up and the phone locked. A four-digit password was needed. He wished everyone would use the Emergency Contact feature on phones. Some people abbreviated it as ICE, a number that could always be called, even from a locked phone. As it turned out, Joe Malinski hadn't set that up. So Ramón had no clue.

In what looked like a small office, he noticed a laptop. After turning it on, he was stumped again with the need for a password. No luck, and he scanned the room. A stack of greeting cards had crashed sideways in de middle of the credenza against the opposing wall. Ramón stepped around the desk and stared at birthday cards and Christmas cards but no envelopes. A top drawer was stuffed with manuals and guides to all sorts of equipment in the house. Warranty cards and small business cards lay strewn amid the reference material.

Another drawer spilled over with cables and old gadgets destined for unknown future use. Turning back, Ramón stared at the desk again where bills and magazines were neatly stacked and concluded that there was nothing here that would turn up an address.

Once in the kitchen area, he didn't see a landline phone where he had hoped to find an address book. Drawers were full of the expected kitchen paraphernalia. The young detective paused and briefly considered taking the cell phone to the coroner's office. He expected the body had been brought in by now. Then he remembered from class that the fingerprint ID on the phone didn't work when the owner was deceased.

His eye fell on the refrigerator, where he noticed a handwritten list stuck to it with a magnet. Bingo. It was titled: *In Case of Emergency*. The items listed were names and numbers of doctors, the hospital, and Brian and Wesley Malinski near the bottom. With addresses and phone numbers. He snapped a picture and walked out through the garage. He opened the car door, got in and discarded the gloves. "All set," he smiled at Lydia. He sent the picture to Travis.

"You got his family info then?"

"Yes. I'm sure your mom is holding dessert for us, and we should be in time for the fireworks!"

***

The spectacle of loud cracks and fireworks was what Ramón and Lydia expected. They sat on a blanket, a small picnic basket between them. The young couple often joined the other spectators near them with the obligatory *oohs* and *aahs* as colorful splashes in the sky lit up the viewing area. Ramón was quite aware that people around them knew him as a policeman. Although their hands touched often, he had convinced Lydia that they needed to avoid any public display of affection. "You mean we can't even kiss on a romantic, fun occasion? People look up at the fireworks, not at us," Lydia had objected, but Ramón remained resolute in his request. As an officer of the law, he felt he needed to show restraint.

It took a while to get out of the heavy traffic after the fireworks, but it was before 11:00 PM when they pulled up to Lydia's home. Only the porch light remained on as it appeared that her family had called it a day and had gone to bed. She wanted Ramón to stay with her for a while, and after turning off the outside light, she grabbed his hand and guided him to sit down on a wide swing.

They hugged and kissed for a short while, and as Lydia gently pushed him away, Ramón knew that his girlfriend had something to discuss. "What's up?" he asked.

"I'm happy we were able to come here for dessert earlier and see the fireworks together," Lydia started. "I'm just not sure we'll have many such evenings like now, especially on a holiday."

"What are you trying to say?"

"I saw you at your job today, and I know what it requires of you. I told you I'm struggling with the hours, and I'm still not sure I can handle that in a relationship."

"Yes, you did say that earlier," Ramón sighed and put his hands on Lydia's shoulders. "I know what you mean, and I understand your concern." He looked her in the eyes and noticed a bit of sadness. Her half-smile added to his anxiety. He feared she wanted to put their relationship on hold or break it off. He knew her concern about his job and the demands it brought with it. He didn't know what she'd heard between Travis and his wife earlier, but it was clear that the future she pictured was different from what she surmised it would be with him. He had to choose his words carefully and put her at ease. He loved this girl and wanted to go on with his plans to buy the engagement ring and marry her. He ever so lightly cleared his throat. "What you saw today may have upset you. I get that. It put the ugly and unsettling part of my job right in your face. I'm sure this won't happen again. I promise I won't bring my work home and will only share the more exciting parts of my job.

Ramón paused, reflecting on what he had just said, curious about Lydia's thoughts. She took a deep breath. "I know you mean that sincerely, Ramón," she said. "As long as you were still an officer, I could count on our planned time together. Now that you're a detective, you and I will never know your hours."

"You're right, Lydia," Ramón said, holding her shoulders firmly. He wanted to pull her closer and hug her, but this conversation needed a positive conclusion. "I'm still a junior detective, and I will have close to normal hours, you know, nine to five. Some cases will require some odd hours once in a while, but don't forget: we don't handle murder cases every day. If my time at the station gets out of hand, I'll make an adjustment. I want to be there for you and with you, whatever we encounter in our lives."

Lydia nodded, and a fuller smile appeared on her face. "You won't hold it against me if I have to remind you of all this in the future?"

"I want you to do that," Ramón said. "Our relationship comes first, and you'll always be my priority. I love you, and I'll always respect your opinion." He raised his eyebrows, surprised he had said what was weighing on his heart.

Lydia leaned in. "Thank you, I love you too," she whispered. They kissed long and tenderly.

Chapter 26

The Sons

The following morning, Travis looked at all the reports from the officers who had canvassed the neighborhood. Nobody had heard a gunshot. It may have been a confusing question to some, given that it had been July 4th and a few neighbors had set off early fireworks. Nobody wanted to make a mistake, or accuse a neighbor by indicating that a gunshot sound had come from a back yard. There were days the wind blew from the direction of the nearby shooting range. Then gunfire was heard all over that neighborhood section. Most people got used to the loud pops and no longer paid attention. Besides that, it appeared to Travis that it was strange that nobody had seen Joe Malinkski walking the trails. He was still waiting for the coroner's report.

Sitting at his desk, Travis held a printout of the picture Ramón had sent in. He called the first son on the list.

"Mr. Malinski, Detective Vinder with the Durham Police Department. My sincere condolences."

"Thanks, Detective." Joe's son said.

"I was also a friend of your dad's; he was my neighbor here in Durham."

"And you're on the case?"

"Yes, I am. I have to keep this short, Mr. Malinski, but I...."

"Please, call me Brian."

"Yes, Brian, I was just checking with you to see whether your Dad shared with you what he was up to the last few months?"

"I don't believe anything special was going on. We talked once a week, you know, about my boys, the weather, his clubs, you know."

"Anything regarding problems in our neighborhood?"

"Nothing that I can recall, Detective. Why?"

"He, your Dad, helped me with a case last year. I couldn't shake the feeling that, even though he was retired, he could easily sink his teeth into something if it needed investigating. We believe that recently he did some investigating into a possible drug smuggling case. Did he mention that, perhaps?"

"He didn't talk about anything like that, Detective. Once he retired from NYPD, he left all that behind, as far as I know. He quit cold turkey."

"Well, he was quite helpful in that case I mentioned. Anyway, I assume then that he didn't discuss any cases with you or your brother."

"Not that I know. So, what drug case was he possibly working on now?"

"I'm not sure he was any longer. All I figure is that he may have been looking into something. He had turned over his findings to the detective in charge. I'm not sure what he was still checking."

"Is that a conclusion based on why or how he was killed?"

Travis paused once he heard the tremble in Brian's voice. It was all too raw, and this conversation wasn't very helpful or supportive. "Listen, Brian. I know that this is hard for you. Your Dad was a good man and a great detective. I really don't have any answers for you at this point."

"I'm sure you'll solve this soon. I believe my brother is flying in tonight. We'll be at the house tomorrow. You can stop by any time to give us an update."

"I'll do that, Brian. I'm going to give your brother a quick call also. See you in a few days. Stay strong."

Travis took a deep breath. It was never easy to have to talk to the victim's family. He had learned not to get too involved. Still, one couldn't help thinking of what that meant to the children or spouse. Grandchildren were denied learning life lessons from another generation. He called Wesley and had pretty much the same conversation he just had with his brother. Nothing stood out, and Joe hadn't shared much about what he might be involved in. Near the end of the short talk, however, Travis got a small glimpse at what Joe was interested in.

"So, he attended a few seminars?"

"That's what he said. He sounded quite passionate about it then. It was months ago."

"Do you remember the topic?"

"Opioid addiction. I remember it clearly because Dad commented on how the drug scene had changed since his days in New York City," Wesley said.

"You're right about that," Travis said. "Did he ever bring it up again since that time?"

"No, Detective. He mostly talked about playing bocce ball, a lady friend who was one of his neighbors, their walks and occasional dates."

"Oh," Travis said. "Did he mention his lady friend's name?"

"He may have at one point, but I can't recall, sorry."

"That's okay," Travis said.

Vinder noted to check out who the lady friend could have been. It sounded like they might have shared what kept them busy daily.

Chapter 27

Mary's Lament

Mary couldn't contain her sobbing. She had an idea why Joe was killed, but would anyone believe her? Joe's body was found under the bridge; how often had she and Joe walked and jogged over that bridge together? With trembling hands, she dialed Durham homicide. After what seemed an eternity, she was patched through to Detective Travis Vinder. "Sit tight, Ms. Valero; we're in the neighborhood and will be there within the hour," the detective had told her.

Mary jumped when her doorbell rang and tried hard to pull herself together and stop crying, all without much success. She invited Detectives Vinder and Acosta into her living room and asked them to take a seat. It took a few minutes and several tissues, but Mary calmed down enough to share her story. "The Spencers next door are responsible. I know it. They are so weird; they must be in witness protection or something."

"Slow down, Ms. Valero, take a deep breath," Vinder calmly responded, "Let's start from the beginning. How do you know Mr. Malinski?"

"Obviously, Joe is my neighbor; he lives two doors down. We're friends, take walks and jog together and share meals. I can't believe he's dead. How can that be? The Spencers live in between Joe and me. They do have so many quirky behaviors. You know Joe is a retired New York City detective. Or was." A sob escaped from Mary.

While Ramón took notes, Travis encouraged Mary to explain what she meant by quirky.

"First, they moved here from The Villages two or three years ago, and this was their second home. They rent here. About three months ago, they sold their home in Florida. Before that, they bounced back and forth between their homes like a yoyo. They hardly had any visitors, didn't belong to clubs, and never socialized. They claim they loved living in The Villages, but they gave that up now. When they moved in next door, I brought them a welcome dinner, and they didn't seem very appreciative. What's the point of living in a place like this if you live like hermits with your blinds drawn? Delivery vehicles come and go, not just the usual Fed Ex and Amazon variety. Many vans and panel trucks pull in the driveway and pull out shortly after." Mary took a few deep breaths before Travis could coax her to continue her narrative.

"One time, Fabio rang my bell and asked to borrow jumper cables because his car wouldn't start. He seemed very nervous, and when I offered to call AAA, his edginess went through the roof, and he practically ran away. That's not a normal reaction to calling AAA, is it?"

"That behavior is indeed odd," is about all Travis could muster. Mary needed to unload. He encouraged her. "So where are they now? Are they home?"

"After they sold their other home, they went missing. I saw them at the airport, really a chance meeting, and they claimed they were flying back to Florida. That was a bunch of bull. Joe quickly found out where they were. In the Caribbean, of all places. St. Maarten."

"I found that out as well," Travis said.

"And they're still there," Ramón added.

"For all I know. Joe had checked into it more because something was very fishy about their behavior."

"How so?" Travis asked.

"It all started when I told Joe about the time I followed Fabio to Durham." She told them that she was the one who saw him one evening at dusk in a bad part of Durham. He was giving several packages to someone with a Camaro. I believe he called you, and then a detective Jackson followed up." She paused briefly and continued: "Joe heard only once from that detective again, and he was a bit upset about that. I know now that involving Joe wasn't my wisest move. About a month before, when the Spencers were still here, I invited Joe over for dinner for the first time. It was back in March and before the neighbor's last round trip to Florida. Joe and I were enjoying dinner on the patio. The Spencers couldn't see us because of my private patio with all the shrubs and the trellis. Joan must have opened her windows to let in the spring breeze. Their windows are never open. Joe and I heard a door slam and angry words exchanged. They were loud, but we couldn't hear much that made sense. Something about *this has to stop, our life is a mess,* and *our granddaughter is better.*"

"So, how did Mr. Malinski react to all this," Ramón asked.

"So, one night, after they'd come back and then went missing, so to speak, he went to the place where we figured they'd made another drop."

"So by that time, you guys figured what? Drugs?"

"Yes. We were sure they were couriers. They lied about their son needing money for his business. Joe did some investigating, and that's why he called you. Detective Jackson, in turn, found out that their money was spent on the medical bills for their granddaughter. That's the last he heard from that detective."

Travis looked up, surprised. Jackson had never shared anything, not that he was obliged to, but having just found out the real story of the money from the Spencers' son, he was confused. "I'll check with Detective Jackson, don't worry. He can probably add to your and Joe's story," Travis said.

Mary continued. "It was the night that Joe spoke to me about the I-95 drug corridor. He strongly advised me not to play Ms. Marple anymore," she said, remembering the concern on his face.

"Joe and I regularly went walking or jogging together after this, mostly in the evening. The Spencers never showed up again, and I kept collecting their mail." She pointed at a large shopping bag sitting by the front door. "Have at it. Who knows what's in there? More secrets, I bet. I have no use for it and wouldn't know where to forward it."

Travis looked at Ramón and motioned with his head toward the bag. Ramón retrieved it and put it by his feet. "So, after you and Joe discovered all that, and don't worry, I'll check what happened with Detective Jackson, were you ever threatened?"

"Sometimes, we sensed we were being followed as we navigated the paths. Still, we never actually saw anyone but fellow joggers. It was always getting dark and cooler when we jogged, very shadowy."

"And Joe didn't investigate further after the detective was involved."

"I don't think so. We just referred to the Spencers as dangerous mules whose contraband possibly killed people. Joe was sure that the hundreds of overdoses resulted from laced drugs in our area. He was sure the drug dealers transported Fentanyl."

Travis stood up and took a deep breath. "Well, Ms. Valero, thank you for this information. You've been most helpful. Please don't hesitate to call Detective Acosta or me if you remember anything else. We may be back to talk to you within the next few days."

Mary sat quietly for a few moments before muttering, "Joe said he'd make sure nobody got hurt. Could that have gotten him killed? Am I in danger?"

Chapter 28

George

George and Betsy were almost home from their trip to Hilton Head where they'd spent a wonderful family weekend with their children and grandchildren. They'd just exited I-540 and were on US-70 when he saw a police car with blinking lights coming up behind him. He asked Betsy, "Was I speeding? Why are we being stopped?" Betsy said, "Maybe you didn't use your turn signal? I got stopped for that a few months ago."

George pulled over to the shoulder and asked Betsy to get the registration card out of the glove compartment while he got his driver's license out of his wallet. He rolled the window down and waited for the officer to approach the car. He handed over his registration card and driver's license and asked, "What's wrong, officer?"

The tall, tanned officer peered into the car and said, "Sir, your license plate is covered with mud. Trying to cover it up, sir?"

George was somewhat startled but said, "No, not at all, Officer. We just got back from Hilton Head where they had heavy rain. The road we took out of our son's rental cottage was extremely muddy. I'll clean the license plate when I get home. I assure you we're not covering anything up."

"Right. For your information, we're patrolling the area, and part of our job is to check all stopped cars, sir," the officer said. "We'll have to search your car."

"Why's that?" Betsy chimed in from the passenger seat.

"It's routine requirement, Ma'am," the officer smiled. "You'll both need to exit the car so we can do a thorough search." George looked at Betsy, and they both sighed and got out of the car.

"Go ahead. Our luggage is in the trunk. I'll push this lever and open it for you. We're not carrying anything illegal or whatever you're looking for."

At that moment, a second police car came along and parked in front of their vehicle. No escaping this squeeze, George thought.

The two policemen searched their car – trunk, reserve tire well, glove compartment, underneath the vehicle, under the hood, under seats, inside their suitcases and side pockets. They found nothing because there was nothing to find, George figured. Ten minutes into the search, it appeared that the car had been searched to the officers' satisfaction.

George couldn't resist and addressed the tall policeman: "Is there some specific reason we were stopped other than the license plate being dirty?"

"You guys are good to go. Just clean off the plate, and you can be on your way."

"But what were you looking for?" George persisted.

"Are you aware that there's a lot of smuggling going on between Florida and states up North?"

"I may have read about that," George agreed.

"Couriers come in all ages. We're checking all cars that we stop for whatever reason. It looks like you live in Durham. It's a destination point for drops of opioids like Fentanyl, shipped from Florida up the east coast to the major cities."

"So, we fit the profile?" George smiled.

"Let me just say that we wouldn't have stopped you if you had a clean license plate," the office grinned.

"I get it," George said as he got back into his car, leaving the door open. "By the way, I've known enough people and families devastated by drug use. I'd like to see all drug traffickers behind bars."

"You and me, both," the officer replied. "You're good to go. Drive safely." He closed the door, and the Benders drove on.

George and Betsy continued the short distance to their home in Carolina Arbors. Betsy said, "From now on, you're on license plate duty!"

George laughed, "Thank God, we only have one!"

Chapter 29

Return

"And by now, Mary and the police know that we sold the house in Florida," Fabio sighed. "Just as we thought it was safe to return."

Before they had time to think of other options, the phone rang. The caller identified himself as Detective Vinder of the Durham Police Department. He told them they were wanted for questioning and should return to Durham immediately. Fabio asked why anyone would think they needed questioning, and Vinder told them it was in their best interest.

"It would be best for you to come home and deal with some issues now before things get worse," said Vinder. "You'll get to tell your side of a story. An event in Carolina Arbors necessitates your urgent cooperation. I suggest you travel back tomorrow at the latest. This will prevent us from having to call the St. Maarten police and send extradition papers. I'm sure you want to avoid the spectacle that would create."

It remained quiet at the small condo where Joan and Fabio had spent the past few months. Travis insisted. "Hello, Mr. Spencer. Did you hear me?"

"Oh, um, yes, I did," Fabio muttered, figuring out why and how they should cooperate. "What event are you talking about, detective?"

"We'll talk about that once you're here," Travis said. "Please make arrangements and call me back with your arrival time."

"We'd be flying into Charlotte."

"That's fine. I want you both to be at the Durham main police station three hours later," Travis said. He gave them his contact information. "Call me within the hour."

Fabio hung up the phone and sank into a chair. Joan looked even more scared. "What was that all about?"

"That was a Detective Vinder from the Durham Police Department. He wasn't precise, but something happened in the neighborhood, and we're to clarify the situation. I have no idea what that is about. Still, he seems aware of what we have done, and I'm sure it will be part of the interrogation. They want us to come back home immediately," replied Fabio.

Joan started to cry, and Fabio held her close. "We don't have a choice. They know where we are, and we can't keep running. Let's go home and deal with whatever charges we face."

Fabio made several calls and arranged the return. He hoped that Mr. Big was no longer looking for them as too much time had passed since they quit. He took a deep breath, called the police station, and confirmed their arrival time.

Fabio hung up the phone with Jason and turned to Joan. "We're in big trouble! The police were looking for us, and the neighbors reported us missing. They talked to Jason. He must have told them we were in St. Maarten. Now, that detective just asked me if someone had given me a package to bring up from Florida." Joan stopped in her tracks and almost screamed. "I can't believe they discovered what we have been doing. How's that possible?"

Fabio took hold of her shoulders and said, "Let's just think for a moment. Did you say anything to one of the neighbors? Did someone see us with a package? Maybe Mary got suspicious after running into us at the airport. I guess disappearing without telling anyone wasn't such a good idea. Maybe we should call Mary. At least that way, no one else in Carolina Arbors will wonder where we are."

"I wonder if Jason told them about Ellie, which means they know we were lying about why we gave him the money."

The next afternoon, the Spencers boarded a direct flight to Charlotte, arriving at 9:00 PM. They spent the night near the airport. Vinder had realized they couldn't make it to Durham as initially required.

"Let's just try to get some sleep and deal with everything in the morning," said Fabio. "Good luck sleeping," was Joan's only reply.

They both tossed and turned all night, and finally, Fabio got up and started to list all the calls he needed to make before their morning flight to RDU. He began with his lawyer friend, who he luckily reached on his first try. The man recommended the firm of Golden, Reynolds & Shore in downtown Durham. He'd call them as soon as their offices opened at 9:00 AM.

The Spencers arrived at RDU Airport around 11:00 AM and picked up their car. They skipped going to their CA home.

He had left a message for Detective Vinder telling him they'd be getting to the police station by noon. Fabio didn't tell Vinder that there'd be a lawyer. He hoped they could meet with their legal counsel before talking with the detective.

On their way to Durham, Fabio called Jason. When their son answered, their son launched into a flood of questions, trying to understand what was going on. "Just let me talk," his father said. "I want to explain everything to you, but for now, just let me tell you the basics. We wanted to help with Ellie's medical expenses, but we didn't tell you where our money came from. We didn't have that much at the time, and we were afraid we'd be unable to fulfill our promise to you and your family. We got an opportunity to make some extra money if we transported some packages between Ocala and Durham every few months. It seemed harmless at first until we realized what we were transporting. We didn't know how to get out of the arrangement, and we were threatened if we tried. We decided to get away for a few months to hopefully figure it all out. Somehow the police found out about our involvement, and now we will be interrogated. I know it sounds like we were very naïve, but it all seemed so harmless at the time."

Jason couldn't believe what he heard, especially since the whole thing happened because they wanted to help his daughter. "Did you get an attorney?" was his first question. "Yes," Fabio responded, "a friend recommended someone, and I already talked with her just before we boarded. She doesn't know much, and we won't talk to the police until we have that attorney with us. It's best to just confess to the whole thing and plead for mercy." Jason agreed and told his father to let him know what happened.

About a minute later, Detective Vinder called and said he'd expect them within the half-hour. He suggested they'd not go home first and come straight to the station. He emphasized that they wanted to avoid being picked up at their home. That would involve an embarrassing scene, including police cars and handcuffs. Fabio assured Detective Vinder they'd already planned to come directly to the station. Once there, they wanted to talk first with a Mrs. Madeline Frazier, who would join them.

"Should we stop somewhere to get a sandwich first?" Joan suggested.

"I don't think we have the time, dear," Fabio answered. "Vinder deemed it imperative that we'd show up at noon. By the time we park downtown, it will be close to that time."

"They must let us talk to the lawyer first, right?" Joan asked.

"Yes. Our earlier conversation was too short. She did sound like a competent attorney. She'll prepare us for the interrogation by the police, and she'll be there with us."

"You know, Fabio, you'll have to do all the talking," said Joan, "I don't think I can deal with this."

Madeline Frazier was a tall blond woman, smartly dressed in a navy blue business suit and a pink silk scarf around her neck. She was waiting for them in a small interrogation room. Vinder had given them thirty minutes to talk, and then he'd join. Fabio was glad they weren't immediately arrested, and things seemed low-key. He and Joan were happy about that but still apprehensive about what might come next. Madeline carried a small leather briefcase. Fabio shook hands with the attorney. "Thanks for coming on such short notice. Let me tell you, we're not criminals, but we do need help with all this."

"We'll see what we can do," Madeline said and motioned the couple to sit down.

The next half hour was spent with Fabio telling her everything about how the transfer of the packages started, why they were doing it and how they were threatened if they tried to stop. One of the major problems was that they didn't know who they were working for. They never met any other couriers. They only met handlers or guys who picked up or gave them boxes or packages. The phone numbers for those guys changed all the time. When Madeline asked Joan if she could add anything, she started to cry and said, "I just wanted to save my granddaughter's life."

Fabio realized he had left out one essential fact. "I forgot to tell you that for some reason, we are also linked to an event that happened in our neighborhood a few days ago. The detective did not share what that was."

"I have a pretty good idea," Madeline said, closing her notepad. "There was a murder of an ex-detective. It has been on the local news for days. No suspect at this point, but it leaked that it might have been related to drug smuggling. I believe we are going to get questions about that."

"We don't have anything to do with that," Fabio replied.

"But you may be, indirectly," Madeline said. "It's not an immediate concern to me as they'd be filing more charges against you. Anyway, we'll find out soon."

"So, what's our strategy?"

"I figure that the detective has plenty of circumstantial evidence against you. They might have some security video of you dealing with your handlers. We will find out. Depending on that evidence, I'll let you answer questions only if I believe that can help the case. Just answer truthfully and stick to the short answer. We don't want to make it worse."

"Okay, I'll do my best," Fabio said.

Before joining the detectives, Madeline discussed the retainer fee and how they'd be required to pay the law firm today.

"I guess I should give you what I can now before the authorities seize our assets. That's a possibility, isn't it?" he asked Madeline.

"Yes," she replied.

Fabio said, "I can write out a check now."

"Fine," Madeline said.

After the transaction, it remained quiet for a few minutes until a knock on the door.

Travis Vinder and Detective Jackson both entered the room. Introductions were made, and Jackson started by officially putting Fabio and Joan under arrest.

"You're under arrest for suspicion of drug trafficking and possible accessory to murder," said Jackson. Joan gasped, and Madeline helped to quiet her down. Jackson continued by reading them their Miranda rights. "You understand these rights as given?" Both Fabio and Joan turned to Madeline, and she said, "Yes."

Malcolm shared a full explanation of the charges in writing, and she quickly reviewed them. Jackson said, "It would help you both if you confess to the drug trafficking and help us track down the dealers in Durham. Then, maybe we can be more lenient on the accessory to the murder charge."

While Madeline continued to look over the paper, Fabio and a quietly weeping Joan sat speechless, facing two stern-looking detectives. After less than half a minute and not waiting for their attorney to comment, Fabio couldn't contain himself anymore. "Who was murdered? We don't know about the murder, and we have nothing to do with that," he said.

"The man murdered is Joe Malinski, your neighbor," Travis said. "He was found July 4th."

Joan jumped up. "No, not Joe. That can't be. He's such a nice man!"

Madeline put her hand on Joan's arm, who sat back down again, tears flowing freely.

"From what we have been told, he was looking into your activities based on information he received from another neighbor. We believe that's why he was killed," Travis said.

"I don't know who the drug dealers are," shouted Fabio. Madeline immediately intervened and gave Fabio a cold stare. She turned to the detectives. "My clients admit to some activities they didn't realize were illegal. That's all," she said. "Murder's not on the table; they haven't been in the state for nearly three months."

"I'll let Detective Vinder deal with the murder element of this case," Malcolm replied, "Let's deal with the smuggling part. I hope your clients will be forthcoming in giving us information on their contacts in Durham and Ocala. I'm looking for full confessions as to their involvement."

"So you'll consider a deal with no jail time?"

"I'll leave that up to the DA. I imagine, though, that jail time is not off the table. Let's get the facts first."

A lengthy conversation ensued with Madeline coloring the Spencers' story in broad strokes of naivete, desperation and the desire to quit the smuggling. She emphasized their overall innocence and culpability. Fabio and Joan added detail where required and wrote down all their drop events in both cities, giving a reasonable description of their handlers. Jackson seemed satisfied for the time being and insisted the couple would spend the night in jail. It was up to Madeline to work out any bail situation the next day in court.

Travis had been following the interrogation without saying a word. Since Jackson seemed to have wrapped up for now on his end, Madeline directed her attention to him.

"What about the accessory to murder charges?"

"We have more work to do on that case before finalizing those charges. It will be up to the DA what to charge your clients with after assessing their indirect involvement in the death of Mr. Malinski."

Fabio and Joan stared in front of them. They became numb as if in shock when they heard they'd be spending time in jail.

Travis continued. "Even though they weren't physically at the Arbors at the time of the murder, we need to check their phones for any contact with the organization. They stand to have benefited from stopping Malinski from investigating your clients' involvement in their smuggling. They didn't want to get caught."

"My clients have already shared all of their contacts in Durham," Madeline stated. "Furthermore, they'd already decided to stop that crazy business. Moving out of the country for three months should indicate that they wanted out and stay away from that gang. They too might have been at risk."

"Yet, it is exactly the risk they took by smuggling that put Mr. Malinski at risk. He paid with his life. Accountability is something we take seriously," Travis said.

"I understand, detective," the attorney said. "I assume that they are not charged with anything involving the murder of their neighbor for now?"

"I still need to get more details about their contacts in Durham. He turned to his colleague. "I think I can take it from here. I'll take them to the booking station when we're finished here."

After Malcolm left, the interrogation continued for another hour. Travis wanted to get every possible detail on their dealings with handlers in Durham and Ocala. He felt that the Spencers possibly knew the murderer or may have seen him. Being stuck in a case was no fun.

The Spencers were hardly listening when their attorney made some arrangements with Travis. Now, the only thing they could do was figure out how to survive a night in jail.

***

Travis hurried to Malcolm's office and slammed the door behind him as he entered to room.

"What the hell is going on?"

Detective Jackson raised his eyebrows. "What are you talking about, Travis?"

"You've been on this case for months! You never shared with me that you talked with Joe, who's now dead, about the drug smuggling. Didn't it cross your mind that Mr. Malinski might have been in danger, having opened the case for you?"

"Wait a minute," Malcolm shot back. "Mr. Malinski was a minor figure in the case I've been working. All he did was provide some possible evidence. Nothing more, certainly not something that would put him in a dangerous situation. I was handling it. Calm down."

"You knew all along that the Spencers were in St. Maarten, right?"

"So? I had no concrete information or proof of their involvement. I knew that at one point, they'd return, and I would question them then. But you seemed to have known more and got them to come back earlier than planned. You didn't share any information with me on that."

"Obviously, this murder case is only a few days old. There was an apparent connection between Joe finding evidence that the Spencers had left behind. You had the same info. I don't understand why you waited for them to return on their own time. Getting them back soon after you knew their whereabouts may have saved Joe's life!" Travis barked.

"I don't see it that way. I was working the case on the drug traffickers, not the mules. I also don't see how I could have prevented Mr. Malinski's murder. We don't even know whether it has anything to do with my case."

"It has everything to do with it!" Travis yelled. "Come on. Don't you see? Bringing the Spencers home earlier would have accelerated your case, getting the contacts in Durham and perhaps in Ocala, and, more importantly, catching a would-be killer or eliminating the need for one. That opportunity was squandered!"

"Listen," Malcolm said as he stood up. "I'll do my job as I see fit. I need to get the big fish. Nobody can tell what happens in that criminal world, and Mr. Malinski could have been a target for another reason. I heard he helped you with another case. Did you ever think someone linked to that case wanted to kill him?"

"That case is over with all principals in jail, and you know it. No, Joe's murder is linked to your case."

"Well, let's do this, Travis. You work your murder case, and I will work the drug case. Now, leave me alone so I can do my job."

Travis didn't think it was worth replying to his colleague. He was going to bring up the possible reaction of the DA on both cases but felt it was for another time. He left the room, again slamming the door shut behind him.

Chapter 30

Follow-up

Travis returned to his office. He was still shaking as he realized it was uncharacteristic of him to fly hot. He had never experienced any issues before with any of the detectives. Maybe he flew off the handle too quickly against Malcolm. He shrugged it off and decided to stick to his case and not bother Malcolm. It was clear to him that the Spencers were essential witnesses in his murder investigation. Malcolm had suggested he'd stick with the narcotic smuggling case and leave the murder case to Vinder and Acosta. *Fine,* he thought. *Hard to deal with someone who doesn't realize that both cases were intertwined through the Spencers.* He sat down as Ramón walked in.

"So, don't you think the timeline over the past three months is an interesting fact we just got from the interrogation? It coincides with the period of involvement by Joe Malinski. Mary had been helpful, and so had the Spencers. For now, I must add. Yet, we have no clue or a lead about the murderer."

Ramón nervously clicked his pen while he sat across from Travis. The annoying repetitiveness of the noise got on Travis's nerves, preventing him from thinking clearly about his next steps. He nodded but didn't say anything.

Ramón, however, used the distraction to force himself to think. He'd never experienced a case in which so little was known. Piecing together the events on the day of the murder was fruitless. Nobody appeared to have seen Joe that day. Quite odd, he thought, because lots of people had been out for the parade earlier, between 11:00 AM and 1:00 PM. If Joe had been outside, his neighbors would have seen him. Even Mary hadn't seen him that day, although they planned to see fireworks at Brier Creek later. Leaving that line of thinking, Ramón suddenly sat up. "Hey, what if that group recruited another couple in the neighborhood? I mean, it's been three months since the Spencers made a run. I can't imagine the handlers would let that happen. That cuts into their profits, and they hate to lose money. What do you think?"

"It's very well possible that there're now newly established couriers, but nothing would lead us to think that this person or persons would live in the CA neighborhood," Vinder said casually, still trying to calm down.

"Okay, just let me ask you this. Would you guess that there's got to be a new courier?"

"And?" Travis asked.

"Well, they'd have to drop off the stuff, right?"

"Yes. I'm sure the traffickers picked a new one. But the likelihood that they choose the same place Mary described to us is small. How are we going to find it?"

"We know the guy picking up the packages from Florida drives a Camaro, right?"

"Yes."

"How about doing a daily patrol for two to three weeks in some of downtown Durham's shadier places? We can do it undercover."

"That would require a lot of cars, looking for just one car one evening. That's like looking for that needle in the haystack, and what if the guy is no longer driving that car?"

"You've got a point there," Ramón sighed. "I was also thinking about the possibility of canvassing a bit in your retirement community to see if we can pick up on other people who are commuting to Florida."

"Again, quite a job, Ramón. But you got me thinking. What if we reversed it? We have someone search for NC license plates seen in The Villages and then track them back to the owners and their residence in North Carolina."

Ramón shook his head. "That's just as hard. Who's going to drive around there, and what if the people there use a Florida license plate?"

Travis was deep in thought for a few moments. He sat up and nodded. "Okay, we'll do our patrols here as suggested. We'll check for shady locations involving a Camero and possibly Florida license plates. That may yield something in Durham."

"And what about Florida?"

"I'll talk to the captain and see if we can get some cooperation. It's probably easy to drive by parking lots at stores in and around The Villages to spot license plates. That's all we need from the uniforms down there. We'll do all the checking here."

"Then we have a plan," Ramón said, leaning back with his chair again.

"It's a long shot, but I believe we should follow it. However, it doesn't get us closer to finding the murderer, so we have more work to do. There's no point in talking with Detective

Jackson at this point. He told me we're both to handle our separate investigations."

"We can't do that without the Spencers, so we need to talk to them again," Ramón said, "I mean, you agree, right?"

"I do, but for now, they've been charged by Malcolm. We'll see how easy it is for us to get access to them when we need them."

"Sounds good," Ramón said. "Also, I was wondering whether we should contact neighbors of the Spencers in Florida. What if they suspected things, or better yet, can shed some info on their behavior?"

"Now, that's just what I've been telling you. That's Malcolm's case, not ours. We need to find a murderer here."

"And what if a killer was sent up from Florida?"

"We'll leave that to Malcolm to discover and tell us." Travis took his empty cup and walked to the coffee corner next to Julia's desk. He motioned for Ramón to come along. Once his cup was filled, they returned to his office.

"So, we have the time of death as noon. The parade was still going on then. We agree that Joe was marched down toward the small creek under the bridge. Most likely at gunpoint. It's so surprising that nobody has seen anything," Travis said.

"Let's assume he took a walk that morning. Remember, he wouldn't have gone with Mary because she was part of the organizing committee for the parade. Check with Mary which path they usually follow and walk it. We will subtract that time from the noon hour to see what time he left. Several homes are near the greenway, so we must check with those neighbors."

"I can do that this morning," Ramón said. "Are we assuming that Joe was jumped just before he was about to cross that bridge?"

"That's indeed my thinking. Also, it's possible that the killer parked his car at a location that wouldn't look suspicious."

"Like the parking lot near the clubhouse?"

"That's a likely place."

"But if it is a normal place, why would people have noticed it?"

"First, we need to find out if it was perhaps a Camaro. That type of car stands out a bit. From the automatic registration log from the visitors' badges, we can find out who was at the clubhouse arriving between ten and eleven that morning. Get some officers to help with that."

"And if it wasn't a Camero?"

"Perhaps a person, I'd say a man, whose's much younger than the average age in the community.

"Would cameras pick him up?"

"I'd have to check with the front desk, but I believe their outdoor cameras are limited."

"I'll check that out while I'm there," Ramón said. "Also, I need to find out how much time it would take from that parking lot to the bridge from the opposite direction Lydia and I walked."

"Good. I didn't look for any hiding places while we were there, but you know the drill. Check all angles. If someone is walking the path toward the bridge, try to position yourself at a point where the person wouldn't see you and where it's only a short distance to the bridge," Travis suggested. "By the way, if you're not back in time for a meeting later with the Captain, don't worry. I'll handle the report so far."

"Fine," Ramón said. "I guess I'll drive over and talk with Mary first. I hope that she and Joe stuck to a usual path. That would make it easier for me."

"It would. If she needs to share more with us, take note. I think she was pretty much in shock when we talked to her, and she might have overlooked signs or can give us a hint, perhaps."

* * *

It was just past ten when Ramón arrived at Mary's house. Not only did she explain where their usual forty-five-minute walk took them, but she also had a map. She handed it to the young detective.

"Now, if we sat down near that big pond near the main road, you can easily add five minutes," she added.

"Joe wouldn't take a break by himself, would he?" Ramón asked.

"Probably not," she sighed.

"Okay, then. I'm going to walk it and see what I find."

"Why don't I come with you, detective?" Mary asked. "This will give you true timing."

"That's fine with me," Ramón answered.

Twenty-four minutes later, they neared the bridge where Joe's body was found. Mary suddenly stopped as it suddenly struck her that she was about to enter the crime scene, the place where her dear friend was killed. She crossed her arms over her chest and turned around, tears flowing freely. Ramón put his hand on her shoulder.

"I'm sorry, Mary," he said quietly.

Mary covered her face with both hands and sobbed. "I don't know why I came here," she said. "What was I thinking?"

"Do you mind staying here for a few secs?" Ramón asked. "I need to check something out."

Mary nodded, and Ramón went into the woods at a place where people had trampled down the grass. He noticed several blackberry bushes ahead of him, possibly explaining the temporary path. It was a good thing all this overgrowth hadn't been cut down. He heard a story at the party where that was a hot issue in the community. He had laughed when he heard that the tall grass could hide snakes that bite dogs. As far as he knew, snakes didn't care; they actually liked the sun once in a while. At any rate, the turned-down grass gave him a clear indication of a short path people had created to get to the blackberry bushes. He turned around and had a good view of the trail while partially hidden. He saw Mary less than thirty feet away and imagined someone using this location as a possible hiding spot. He looked around on the ground and spotted two stepped-on cigarette butts. He smiled, retrieved a small plastic evidence bag, and scooted the butts into it with a small stick. He checked for any other objects, but finding none, he briskly walked over to Mary. That took less than five seconds.

"Okay, Mary," he said. "Let's get out of here."

They quickly crossed the wooden bridge as Mary held her hand in front of her mouth. Once on the street, she took a deep breath. "I don't think I can ever walk here again," she said, wiping her eyes. "He was such a good man."

"Let's go to your house the shortest way," Ramón suggested. "I need to get my car and go to the clubhouse to gather more information."

"Are you and the other detective any closer?" Mary asked, pointing in the direction of another part of the trail.

"We don't have a suspect at this time if that's what you're asking," he answered. "We are making some progress on the how and when. That may eventually lead to a suspect."

"Good," Mary said.

They walked the rest of the way without saying a word. At the house, Ramón said goodbye and agreed to let her know if she could be of more help. He made his way to the clubhouse.

***

As Ramón walked into Piedmont Hall, his phone rang.

"Hey Lydia," he said, making an immediate U-turn and walking back outside. "What's up?"

"Not much, just on my lunch break, wondering whether I will see you tonight."

"I told you I'm working nine to five for sure. It's looking good so far," he smiled. "Where would you like to go? Dinner and a movie? There're some new action movies I'd like to see with you."

"We can do that," she said. "But what about the case? Are you any closer to finding who murdered that man?"

"Not much, I'm afraid. I'm looking into possible witnesses who may have seen the unsub if he parked his car in the clubhouse parking lot."

"Why do you think it was a man?"

"By stats, most crimes like this a committed by a male. Given the strength and force used to get the victim down under the bridge, we believe it's a man."

"Or a strong woman?"

"Lydia, it's my first case as a junior detective. Give me some slack, girl," he laughed. "Anyway, I'm going on what I learned, and this case fits a male suspect."

"Just messing with you, Ramón," she said, laughing. "Anyway, see you at 6:30?"

"Great, unless something pops up at my end, of course. You go ahead and pick the restaurant in Raleigh."

"Nothing will pop up! Love to find a fun place to eat. Ciao," Lydia said and ended the call.

Ramón headed back inside the clubhouse. He was gladly surprised when he discovered that one outdoor camera was looking at the western part of the parking lot. He viewed the recording of July 4th between 10:00 AM and 12:30 PM with the manager. Most people they observed parking at that end of the lot were pickleball and tennis players. At the 10:15 mark, an old white BMW parked near the second entrance. The man getting out wore khaki pants and a black t-shirt and was most likely in his forties, Ramón figured. The man closed the door, took a last drag on a cigarette, and threw the butt on the ground, stomping it with his foot. Ramón pointed at the screen.

"Can you freeze this?"

The manager stopped the video. "Do you want a snapshot of this?" he asked

"Yes, please," Ramón answered. "Can you zoom in on the man?"

"It's not very clear, to begin with," the manager answered, "but I can try."

The picture quickly became fuzzy and didn't seem to help much as the man wasn't facing the camera straight on."

"Don't worry; we can do some enhancement at the station if this is a person of interest."

"I'll copy the zoomed-in version then," the manager said.

They continued watching the man who already had a mask on. It didn't seem like he locked the car as he walked away, past the pickleball courts and disappeared towards the trail.

"Let's rewind this and see it in slow-mo," Ramón requested.

The manager took a few more snapshots, including a close-up of the car and the man walking. No license tag was visible, and the man was seen putting on sunglasses.

"I'll take the video with me," Ramón said. "Does it contain a recording till about 1:00 PM?"

"It goes till the end of the day," the manager responded. By the way, I can upload the video to our website, so you don't need to take it with you. Here is the link."

The manager wrote down the entire URL and handed it to the detective with a half dozen pictures. Once outside, Ramón dropped the 8x11 images onto the passenger seat of his car and walked over to the spot where he'd seen the car. He searched for a cigarette butt. He spotted no such thing in the immediate area and figured the wind must have blown it away. He walked methodically through the whole western part of the parking lot and found six butts he bagged separately. Two were clearly stepped on. The others barely had the filter and looked weathered.

Ramón took snapshots of the pictures and sent them to Travis. Feeling good about having very likely seen the person of interest, he couldn't wait to head back to the station. No need to canvas the residents who had been to the center that morning. He felt he had more than he had hoped for.

Chapter 31

Reaching Out

Travis felt good about the information he'd gathered from the Spencers and their Carolina Arbors neighbors. He was certainly more aware of the drug courier operations, although not close enough to identify Joe Malinski's murderer. Given the intent to check out Florida license plates in Durham, he realized that more information was needed on why Joe had become a threat. After Ramón had left, he'd gotten access to the Spencers without involving Malcolm. That was good to know. The couple hadn't asked for their lawyer, which was another plus. He asked them for the names of their neighbors in The Villages for two purposes. First, he wanted someone who could corroborate their story, and second, Travis needed someone who would share how the Spencers behaved over the past two years. Perhaps they, too, had seen something. Not that he was intent on helping Malcolm. Knowing a bit more about who they interacted with there may lead to someone who might travel up north. Perhaps a killer, as Ramón had suggested.

The couple had divulged the name and phone number of Susan Hillendale, a next-door neighbor, and Travis felt it could be a good start. He had set up a call to find out anything Susan could share. The phone rang.

"Hello, Susan here," Mrs. Hillendale said.

"Detective Travis Vinder with the Durham Police Department in Carolina," Travis introduced himself. "Thanks for taking my call. I'll keep it brief. You're not in any trouble; rest assured. I'm gathering information for a case here. All I want is to talk about your neighbors, the Spencers."

"Oh, well, that's fine," Susan replied. "What can I help you with, detective? You know they don't live here anymore, right?"

"Yes, I do. Tell me a bit about their behavior over the past two years," Travis started.

"They're in trouble, aren't they?" Susan said.

"Well, we are holding them in a case we're working on. But tell me, did you notice any changes in the Spencers?"

"Well, you see, things were not like in the beginning when we were neighbors. They started acting differently, and it always puzzled me."

"And how would you describe this changed behavior that made you suspicious, Mrs. Hillendale?"

"Just their tuning out to the community, frequent trips up north, and minimal contact with neighbors. And then there were their secrets."

"Oh, tell me about that."

"So, one evening, after I overheard them discussing a drop-off, I followed Fabio. He met someone in Ocala. I took a few pictures of the meetup that night." Susan took a deep breath. Travis didn't interrupt her. From his many years of police work, he knew that when a person voluntarily came forward with a complaint against someone, it was usually because they had a vendetta against that person. Was Susan upset with Fabio for some reason? Why would she follow him, particularly at night? He wasn't even sure that her information was helpful. He waited patiently, and she went on about the road she took.

"You know, detective, they traveled back and forth between Florida and North Carolina, never giving me a notice on what day they'd leave or be back. I mean, I was picking up their mail, and they just assumed I would check if it filled up after a few days."

Travis nodded, took a few notes, and put the call on speakerphone.

"As I said, they kept to themselves more and no longer participated in community activities. And not seeing their son or other family members visiting here was odd. But the icing on the cake – so to speak – was that loud argument I overheard. That's when all of my suspicions were confirmed."

"You've mentioned that twice now," Travis said. "What did you hear?"

"First, Joan said they had no choice but to move and that they had to stop doing whatever they were doing. They then talked about somebody they called the Big Boss and how he would prevent them from stopping. My ears burned when they mentioned a meeting the next night at 9:00 PM. It was then that I knew I had to follow Fabio and get to the bottom of what they were up to," said Susan.

"And you didn't talk to them about what you heard?" Travis asked.

"No, I tried to talk to Joan before, but she avoided my questions. It was always the same excuse: going to see their son and help with his business and family."

"Okay," Travis interjected to encourage her to share more of her story.

"So, that evening, I walked around the block several times and saw Fabio take his golf clubs out of the trunk of his car. He put in a large black blanket. I thought that was strange."

Ramón coughed lightly. "So he took off right away?" he asked.

"He did, and I followed him to a small strip mall in Ocala," Susan eagerly confided. "I watched Fabio back his car into a spot and turn off his headlights. Then, a dark sedan pulled up next to his Equinox. A short, stocky Hispanic-looking man with a mustache got out of the sedan. Fabio stepped out of his car, and the man handed Fabio several smaller packages wrapped in black plastic. Fabio stuffed them all against the back of the seat and then covered them with the blanket. Some packages disappeared under the front seats, I think. The whole thing looked like an illicit business transaction! But I don't know what was in the packages, and I'm itching to find out." Susan paused as if she were waiting for a comment. When none was forthcoming, she continued.

"I had brought my phone in the car and took a few pictures, and I zoomed in for some of them. But those close-ups were blurry – I was just too far away. Worse, the license plates weren't clearly visible."

"Just email me the pictures, even the blurry ones," Travis said as he gave her his email address. "Perhaps, there's something forensics can do with that. Did you see anything else?"

"I then noticed Fabio and the Hispanic man arguing. The man moved closer to Fabio and stabbed his finger in my neighbor's chest several times. They both looked angry, and Fabio got into his car and drove away. This is the most exciting thing I've ever done in my life. Still, after witnessing this, I was a nervous wreck, so I went to my favorite restaurant in Ocala and had something to eat to calm myself down."

"Detective work is hard," Travis chuckled. "Those pictures are essential to us. They'll also give us a time and place where you took them. Don't worry about the license plate numbers. The time-stamp will help us find the cars from surveillance tapes on nearby traffic cameras.

"Oh, good. I'm sending the pictures right now," Susan said.

Travis briefly thought about giving her Malcolm's email but decided not to. "Thanks," he said. "We appreciate what you've done. I suggest you don't do that in the future. You put yourself in danger, and your local law enforcement is better at handling this kind of stakeout. Anyway, it turned out okay, so thanks again."

"You're welcome," Susan said and ended the call.

***

Later that afternoon, Ramón returned and had the lab deal with the cigarette butts he had found. He walked into Travis' office, who briefed him on his conversation with Susan.

"Well, that was crazy for her to follow him at night like that," Ramón remarked. 'By the way, I'd like to see the pictures."

"Her story adds a parallel dimension to this case, and I'm glad we could get so much information from her. Let's see where it leads," said Travis.

"So, I talked with Mary, who, by the way, is still very upset. She did take me on the walk I was hoping for. It's put a definite timeline in the case, assuming Joe walked from his home straight for the path and then on to the bridge. I'll update the chart," Ramón said. "Did you get her email yet?"

Travis shook his head. "I hope she reduced the size of the pictures a little. She may have difficulty sending them all simultaneously as attachments to one email."

"True," Ramón agreed. "Also, I went to the clubhouse. We have some pictures here of our possible suspect. I already sent them to forensics."

He put the pictures on the desk, and Travis stared at them intently. Each photo had a time stamp on it.

"And the white BMW is his car then," Travis said. "Good work."

"Here's the URL to download the whole recording of the parking lot on the western side for that day. Perhaps we should pass this on to forensics?"

"I'll do that," Travis said.

"Oh, and on the way over here, I was thinking. How about getting them to look for that car on recordings by nearby traffic cameras, if there are any? They should be within a few miles and have something around 11:00 AM."

"Well, they'll have their work cut out. Let's see also whether the man with the BMW matches any pictures from Florida. You never know."

Travis' phone was buzzing. He took the call and said *Okay, any time now is fine.*

"That's one of my neighbors," Travis volunteered. "Take all this to the lab. Tell them I'll forward the email from the lady in Florida. You can spend the rest of the day with forensics if possible. Again, good work, Ramón," Travis said.

Chapter 32

George's Input

George entered Detective Vinder's office, shook hands, and sat down.

"How have you been, George?" Travis asked.

"Not bad. Thanks for seeing me on such short notice."

"No problem. What's on your mind?"

"I haven't talked to anyone about this, except for my wife, of course, but I have anecdotal evidence that our neighborhood friends are increasingly susceptible to improper use of opioids or even illegal drugs."

"That's possible, but you know that this isn't my beat."

"Granted, but I'd like to tell you why I wanted to talk with you."

"Okay, go ahead, George," Travis said.

"When I got stopped yesterday by the police, I was a possible suspect in smuggling drugs into our neighborhood for a short moment. At least, that's what the policeman indicated. Frankly, I was unaware of the drug trafficking of opioids along Interstate 95 or any other highway. I was rather shocked by the incident and even more so when I got home and heard about Joe's death. He was a member of our Men's Club."

"I know," Travis said. "This is a sad case."

"Anything we can help with? I mean, our sleuths club? Was Joe involved in something? Was it drugs? What can you tell me?"

Travis said, "I appreciate the offer, but I can't disclose much. We know there may be a link to something you just mentioned: drug smuggling. Pretty much like the officer who stopped you said. This is a dangerous business. Mules are facing pressure from the gangs as well as from law enforcement. What, if anything, do you know about drug use in our neighborhood?"

"Betsy and I talked about that last night. We've not seen any obvious cases of drug use or overdoses. However, we heard of a son staying with his parents here, and he overdosed one evening. He's fine now. With people of our age, diseases such as cancer or arthritis, and lots of operations on knees and shoulders, it wouldn't surprise me if there were many painkiller users around us. We have several Vietnam veterans in our neighborhood. Several have issues such as PTSD or suffer from the effects of Agent Orange. Nothing would surprise me except for the smuggling itself."

"Have you or Betsy ever used any opioids?"

"When my gall bladder was removed four years ago, I was given ten oxycodone tablets. I took a few for pain relief but didn't feel much relief or why people find them addictive. I threw away most of the pills. Maybe they weren't as strong as the ones you get from smugglers. Fortunately, my experience with drugs is limited other than seeing the impact of drugs on other people's lives – which is bad enough."

Travis asked, "Do you think the Sleuths might be able to add any insights to our investigation?"

"Maybe, but there's a person in our group who was a nurse. She's what's called an expert in harm reduction and the irresponsible use of drugs. At least that's what I remember."

"Do you have her number?"

George showed his phone to Travis. "This is Barbara's number." While Travis wrote down the number, George continued. "To answer your earlier question, we have a meeting in a few days. I can send out a note to the members telling them you'll be there and want to ask them about opioid usage in the Arbors. I'm pretty sure you'll get some interesting feedback from not only Barbara."

"Thank you, that would be helpful. I'll see you then – 3:00 PM on Thursday, right?"

"You got it. By the way, I did wash my license plate. That's why we were stopped: a dirty license tag! I'm so paranoid about this. I look at my license plate before getting in my car every time now!"

Chapter 33

Joe's Last Days

It was mid-afternoon when Ramón got a call from one of Joe's neighbors. He left the forensics lab as they were still working on face enhancements and walked to his own office. Mark Turnbull was a member of the Sleuths book club and had talked earlier with George Bender. "I couldn't reach detective Vinder, and I was referred to you," Mark said. "We've met before during a few cases, as you have come over to our book club a few times."

Ramón couldn't picture the man but agreed anyway. "Oh, sure, yes," he said. "What can I help you with today?"

"Well, I think I'm the one who may help you in this case," Mark said. "You see, I talked with Joe last week, and he told me a few things which didn't make sense then, but they do now."

"How so?"

"A few months ago, I was at a lecture about drug use, both legal and illegal substances. It was held in our clubhouse, and Joe was there too."

"I see," Ramón said as he was taking notes. "Did you get to speak with Joe about that?"

"Yes, I did. All he talked about was how the illegal drugs were being smuggled into our community."

"You mean to say he knew about smuggling?"

"He had a feeling it was happening. Not that there were users in our community, but he was sure there was a market in the Triangle community."

"Did he say anything about knowing smugglers?"

"No, but he figured people in our community who acted as snowbirds would be the perfect mules. Of course, I asked him if he had any suspicions. He remained elusive and commented that it may be people who you least expect."

"Obviously, that talk had given him some ideas he wanted to follow up on?"

"Knowing Joe and his previous job, I'm sure he did. You see, once he researched something, he didn't let go. He did mention his neighbor Mary. You see, he had become good friends with her, both being single. She wasn't involved, but she was concerned about the danger of these drugs in our community."

"I see," Ramón said. He did have another question for Mark. "When's the last time you saw Joe?"

"Let's see, that was Saturday at the gym. So, just a few days ago."

"Did you talk with him?"

"Just briefly about the Bocce Ball Club championship in about three weeks."

"And, he was looking forward to that?"

"Oh yes."

"Anything else?"

Mark was quiet for a few moments and then had what seemed an *Aha*'moment. "Now that you ask. He then said that he had seen a guy staring at him while he played bocce ball the day before. That would have been on Friday morning. First, he thought it was a player from another Del Webb community who came out to stake out the caliber of players in our club. We sometimes invite players from other 55+ communities. Then he told me that the man was only looking at him."

"Did he describe that person?"

"No, he didn't, and he didn't elaborate any further."

"So, you're telling us that Joe was concerned about drug runners and drug use."

"I'd say that was his interest."

"Well, Mr. Turnbull, thanks for your call. If there's anything else you recall, let us know. I heard from Detective Vinder, and I'll visit you during the book club meeting on Thursday. That would be a good time to share more info if you have anything."

"Ok, see you then," Mark said and hung up.

Ramón finished adding something to his notes. The main thing he took away from the conversation with Mark was about the man who possibly stalked Joe. He needed to call the manager at the clubhouse and give him a link to the videos from last Friday. If the car and the man were there again, it would confirm that Joe was being followed. And that it had to do with his private investigation of drug smuggling in the neighborhood was a sure thing.

Ramón stopped by Travis's desk. The detective was studying the pictures that Susan had sent. He looked up. "Do you have something?" he asked, pushing back his chair while taking his reader glasses off.

"I think someone singled out Joe."

"The killer?"

"I'm guessing, but I'll check with the clubhouse manager. He can send me another link, maybe this time from the parking lot and the back where the bocce ball courts are. I believe I need the recordings from July 3rd between 9:00 and 11:00 AM. That should do it. I'll be going over them as soon as I get access. After that, I'm calling it a day, if that's okay with you."

"Sure. Now, if we find the same person we saw on the fourth, we can hope for a better picture of the killer this time. By the way, anything on those cigarette butts?"

"Oh, yes, I almost forgot. They got a partial DNA match between the ones from the possible hiding place near the bridge and the one in the parking lot."

"Well, that confirms our train of thought. The killer smokes, and he squashes his butts on the ground."

"I'll add it to the board," Ramón said. "By the way, what are you looking at?"

"These are Susan's pictures. The ones from Ocala. I recognize Fabio Spencer, but the handler is a job for the police there. They may just recognize him. I'm about to run his image through the facial recognition program."

"I don't think identifying him will bring us closer to Joe's killer," Ramón said. "Joe obviously only relied on information he gathered here in Durham. I think that's the part of the network that will get us closer."

"Oh, I don't disagree with you," Travis smiled, putting on his glasses. "I may pass this along to detective Jackson, although I'm not sure I want to meddle in his investigation if you know what I mean,' Travis said sarcastically, using two-finger quotes.

"Got it," Ramón frowned. "I'll be in my office. I hope to see that white BMW again in the video."

"Good. I hope your hunch about the same guy staking out the victim is confirmed."

***

Ramón looked at the morning video, starting at the 9:00 AM timestamp on the previous Friday. At that time, the white BMW was already in the parking lot. A minor rewind revealed the same character getting out of the car. This time the unsub didn't put on a mask as he walked toward the pickleball and tennis courts. The bocce ball courts were just around the corner.

The man looked again to be about forty, blond and a bodybuilder. The description of 'enforcer' came to Ramón's mind. Enforcing what? Keeping the secret of drug smuggling and protecting the people involved? Preventing others from meddling in their business? Killing anyone on the trail of these illegal activities? Ramón strongly felt that one of those answers would come back in the affirmative soon.

He made a few prints from the video and continued to search the recording, this time from the back of the clubhouse. He was disappointed, as the angle of the camera wasn't ideal. While he saw a man's legs standing between the tennis courts and the bocce ball courts, the trees obstructed the torso. He waited patiently until the man moved away ten minutes later. This time he had his back to the camera and most likely was heading to his car.

Ramón returned to the recording showing the parking lot, knowing the exact time he needed to look: 9:28 AM. And just like clockwork, the suspect sauntered toward his BMW, stopping briefly to stare at the pickleball courts. Then unaware of the camera or careless, he reached his car. His face was uncovered, and when he took off his sunglasses to wipe his forehead with his left arm, Ramón took a snapshot. "Gotcha," he said. "Now, who are you?"

He continued watching until the car drove off, but a few trees obscured the license plate, and then suddenly, it was too far to make out the letters and numbers. He checked his watch. Perfect. Lydia would be happy.

Chapter 34

The Vinders

With the identity of the murderer still elusive, Travis went home around 6:00 PM. He faintly expected to smell dinner cooking as he walked in, but the short hallway was odor-free and quiet. A few *Hellos* remained unanswered. In the kitchen, he spotted a note on the kitchen counter.

"You're on your own," he read. *"Will be back at 10:00 PM."*

Travis crumbled up the paper and threw it in the garbage. He pulled a beer from the fridge and paced around the kitchen for a while, taking large swigs regularly until the bottle was empty. He wasn't about to start cooking. He briefly wondered where Maureen had gone but then shrugged his shoulders. He wouldn't have to talk to her if she wasn't around because all she did lately was nag him. He was so over it. And then the stupid argument on the 4th. Everything was going well; the guests had a great time and a few too many drinks. At first, he didn't notice her, but a volleyball game started at one point, and Julia was standing next to him. Having no desire to play, he put his arm around Julia's waist to push her towards the makeshift play area.

She resisted, and it may have looked like he was hanging on to her. To make matters worse, he later thought, the harder he pushed, the more she moved closer to him. That's all Maureen had seen, and the lid had come off.

He shook his head. He couldn't blame Julia. It was all his fault, yet nothing was meant by it. He didn't deny that he liked her. Still, he always handled any situation in the detectives' offices properly. There had been mandatory meetings explaining inappropriate behavior, bullying and so on, and everyone was quite aware that those kinds of things did not belong in any workplace. But this was different. Although his arm movement had started innocently enough when her body touched his, and she looked at him with a big smile and sparkling eyes, perhaps she had a smidgen too much to drink, he had felt a titillating twinge throughout his body. That, too, was on him. When they'd gone out with the team in the past, she always sat next to him, and he liked it. There'd never been any physical contact he was aware of or remembered. Even though they'd put quite a few drinks away, he was pretty sure nothing ever happened. Now that was all different. It was at his home, in front of Maureen. He doubted anyone else had seen it, so it was unfortunate that his wife was the one who did!

Their conversation in the kitchen had quickly escalated. Where in the past, Maureen made some insinuations upon her return from spending months with her ailing father in Philadelphia, it now seemed to her that she was proven right all along. The funny thing was, he never was close to Julia again, as the party was interrupted by the new murder case. Maureen had said some mean things. It seemed like she'd just proven a point that had been on her mind for a long time but never expressed out loud to him. What could he say to convince her that nothing was going on between him and his assistant? If Maureen wanted to think that, there wasn't much he could say. If something were going on, he would have had to report it to his superiors, and soon the whole force would know. Also, Julia could have filed a complaint in the past if he had made any unwanted advances toward her. That simply was pure speculation because nothing happened. Period.

Travis finished another beer and decided a walk would do him good. It took him over twenty minutes to go to the Bad Daddy's Burger restaurant at Brier Creek. He ordered a loaded burger and a portion of truffle fries. He slowly ate his meal while staring at people coming and going, imagining what they did in life and whether they were happy. It was nearly 9:30 PM when he returned home. He had gone over what he was going to say multiple times. He hoped Maureen would listen to him and see that there was no reason to think their marriage was in trouble. Perhaps something else was going on at her end. Something he wasn't aware of. He'd have to listen patiently to her as well.

He turned on the TV in the family room and looked for her favorite station: The Hallmark Channel. He didn't care for all the soapy stories, the sudden heartbreaks and the prince on a white stallion to the rescue in the end. He swore that the episode featured the same actors he'd seen before in one or more other stories he had happened upon while Maureen was watching. He hoped the show would put her in a better mood when she walked in. Then again, he had no idea where she'd gone and in what state she was coming home.

Twenty minutes into the episode, he heard the garage door opening. He straightened up from his favorite slouch position in the corner of the sofa. Maureen walked in, throwing her purse and keys on the kitchen counter. "Ah, you're still up, I see," she snarled, indicating her mood. Travis stood up. She didn't wait for a reply as she took off to the half-bath. Moments later, she appeared, straightening a skirt that didn't need it.

"So, what did you have for dinner," she started.

"I figured you went out for dinner, so I walked over to Bad Daddy's," he said. "Where did you go?"

"I guess we were close. We did the Ale House with a few neighbors. Anyway, I'm tired. I'm going to bed."

"Can we talk first for a while," Travis offered.

"There isn't much to talk about, now, is there?" Maureen said, making her way to the master bedroom.

"Yes, there is," he said, cutting her off. "Why don't we sit down on the couch? There's something I need to tell you," Travis said, having rehearsed that earlier. He knew that something new might interest her. It worked.

"Okay," Maureen said and sat down. "What's up?"

"Well, I gather I need to come clean about something," he started.

"About time." She ran the palm of her hand across her lap as if to flatten the skirt again.

"It's about us."

"Oh, is there something new?"

"I believe I may have taken you for granted the past few months, and I don't think I've been listening well. I've been busy with cases, but that's nothing new. Also, that's not an excuse."

"And?"

"We've just grown apart, I think, and we have been thinking our own thoughts and not sharing them like we used to."

"And what are you thinking, or what do you think I'm thinking about?" Maureen asked, glancing at the TV, not even looking at Travis.

"I feel that you don't trust me, that I'm unfaithful, and that I have fallen out of love." "Do you mind if I turn that off for now?" He picked up the remote.

"Go ahead," Maureen said, this time looking at him. "So, you're telling me that the fling you had or have with Julia doesn't mean anything? Honey, you're not fooling anyone. Least of all me."

"That's exactly what I'm trying to say to you. There's nothing between her and me, Nothing. If there were, I'd have been kicked off the force. There is no tolerance for that kind of relationship at the station."

"You know you spent all afternoon near her, and I know how she always looks at you. There's something, Travis. Something you're not telling me."

"I can't keep her from doing what she thinks she can do, but I wasn't aware of what you're saying. Not at all."

"And grabbing and pulling her close to you was also her doing? Everyone saw that. It was so embarrassing, shameless. What do you think people figure is going on?"

"I pushed her toward the game that was starting. She held back and turned into me. If you saw that, you saw me walk away too. You've got to have seen that."

"I think you realized what you'd done in front of everyone and quickly put some space between the two of you."

"Oh, I realized what she'd done, and I'd have none of it. She had too much to drink."

"Travis, you can explain many things, but I can see it in your eyes. When you talk about her, you're very defensive toward me but always forgiving toward her. When you speak of her, your eyes light up. I know because I know you."

"Yet, there's nothing between us, never has been, never will. You're my wife, and I should pay more attention to you."

"Listen, it's late, and I need to sleep. Think about what you said. Maybe we'll have a different conversation tomorrow."

"But I don't want to keep rehashing this, Maureen. I love you and nobody else. I know things are on your mind, but I don't know what they are. I want to know. If something's bothering you, I want to know. If you need help, I want to offer it. We should talk more about what's going on in your life than mine. I want to keep my job, so I must be honest and professional. Tell me, is there anything that's upsetting you?"

Maureen looked away. He thought he'd seen a tear in her eyes. Was there something wrong? Was she pushing him away and using a trumped-up relationship as an excuse? He instantly felt that he wasn't a good detective after all if he couldn't solve the case of his own marriage. What the hell? He didn't know what to say, so he reached to touch her hand. Maureen flinched and put her hands in her lap, still not looking at him. It remained quiet for the longest time. Travis moved closer and put a hand on her shoulder. Slowly, Maureen turned to him, and there were more tears. She took a deep breath. "I'm sorry, Travis, but I believe I have fallen out of love with you. It's not something I can explain, but..."

"What did I..." he cut in and then realized that he had promised himself he'd listen. "Go on..."

Maureen hadn't moved. "It started in Philadelphia. It was miserable being my Dad's main caregiver. My brother was of no use, and all the heavy lifting was up to me. Slowly I overcame all the obstacles and realized I wanted to be alone. I could handle life on my own. I wanted to go somewhere, on a big vacation, not back to Durham and this place where all my neighbors are my Dad's age. When I came back, I saw that you, too, had grown to be independent. It was six months. That's all it took. You talked about your assistant as if she pulled you through during my absence while I had to go through it alone. I don't want this life. I need to feel wanted in a place where I can enjoy life, a beach, a forest, a mountain, anywhere but in a retirement community. I'm not happy here, and we have our own lives."

She paused, and although Travis was ready to counter her arguments, he bit his lip and stayed quiet. He realized that there was more to come.

"So, I grew happy for you in a way, knowing that you had someone. Or maybe, I wished for it. It would make it so much easier to walk away and leave. When I saw you at the party with her, I was mad because I realized that it may all come true, and I'm not sure I'm ready." She got up and took a tissue from the box on the counter. She blew her nose and coughed before sitting back down.

"Why didn't you tell me this before, Maureen," Travis said softly. "We had such a good relationship; we always talked things through even when we couldn't have the family we always wanted. I'm here for you. You know that. We can fix whatever you think needs fixing. That includes moving. I'd do that with you and for you."

Maureen nodded. There were more tears. "I understand that, but I'm very unsure right now. About you, about us." She stood up and took another tissue. "I need to go to bed now. Maybe we'll talk tomorrow."

Travis stood up as well. "I hope you sleep well. I care about you and love you. I'll be there in a while."

After Maureen left, Travis sat back on the couch, his mind racing with all sorts of ideas, solutions, vacation plans, moving and many other things that his wife had said. He went to bed later, and for the first time in years, he didn't think about a case as he fell asleep.

Chapter 35

Morning Joe

The following day when Ramón walked in, Travis was staring at mugshots on a large screen. To his right, he noticed the whiteboard where the detective had written on, taped pictures, and drawn lines. It mimicked a timeline starting a year ago when the Spencers were moving drugs and money. At the three months ago mark, a vertical set of pictures showed Joe, Mary, and the location in Durham labeled as the drop zone. The July 4th mark had the now clear image of the suspect. No name had been written below it yet. A line ran from the drop zone to the word *Contact,* and another ran to the word *Cash*. A line from Joe went to a good picture of the suspect. Below he read *White BMW* and *cigarette butts*. Overall, Ramón thought it was a sparse representation of the case.

"Ah, Ramón," Travis said. "Thanks for a better picture of the murderer."

"Are you doing facial recognition?"

"We're running his picture through the database, but nothing's turned up yet. I'm checking some photos from our surveillance teams over the past few years. No luck yet."

"Do you believe it's someone from the Durham area?"

"Not sure, but we can't leave a stone unturned."

"Wouldn't the drug dealers hire someone from out of town to do their dirty work?"

"I'm leaning that way," Travis nodded. "After all, a quick visit of an assassin looks to me like how they'd run it. I suspect that the network that manages the drug couriers and the distribution operation has many operators," he continued. "I've talked with the captain, and the anti-drug squad has been monitoring several bits and pieces of activities but have never been able to trace the action. With this case, we have a lot more. The Spencers are one set of mules, and they can recognize their handlers or contacts in Durham and Ocala. The captain suspects there're more couriers because more and more drugs are coming up from Florida."

"How does he know," Ramón asked.

"The number of overdoses in our county and the state. Fentanyl is getting through profusely and wreaking havoc in our community. I wish we had pictures of a drop. It would lead us to an arrest with proof, and we could put the squeeze on the handler, which may lead us further up the organization. We now have a description that fits nobody and a picture of someone we don't know. Frustrating. I still think the murderer is part of the cell operating in our area."

"Be that as it may," Ramón sighed, "as long as we don't know who this is, we can't search for him."

"Have you searched for his car?" Ramón asked. "I mean, we don't have the plates, but we have the make and color of it."

"We're working on that. We're not even sure it's a car registered in North Carolina. Right now, we have over five hundred cars that fit that type. An impossible task to track them all down."

"Well, I don't mind checking on those in Durham County," Ramón offered.

"It's already being done," Travis said. "That's the least we could do. The traffic cams are still being studied."

"And no results yet," Ramón offered.

"Correct. We're not sure expanding into adjoining counties would yield anything," Travis said. He turned back toward the screen as his phone rang. It was Malcolm. He put the call on speaker phone.

"Yeah, what's up?"

"I get what you said yesterday, but I believe we need to work this SOB case together," Malcolm said. "I heard you spoke with the Spencers, and we need to be on the same page here. What do you say?"

Travis cleared his throat. "So, you do agree then that both cases are intertwined."

"I thought about it, and I agree, but the timing of the killing of your friend Joe doesn't fit in my timeline nor in the purview of my investigation."

"I disagree, but I realize we must put our heads together. The best outcome would be that you get the put the drug gang away, and we get our killer."

"Good," Malcolm said. "I'll be over in a minute."

The call ended, and Travis sighed. "I swear he'll have to admit at some point that Joe's murder could have been prevented. Narcs are a different breed, that's for sure." He noticed that Ramón rolled his eyes. He was about to say something when the young detective's phone rang.

Ramón smiled and shook his head. It was Lydia, but he felt he had to stay with work.

"Go ahead, take it," Travis said as he turned toward the mugshots flashing across the screen.

"Hi Lydia," Ramón said as he walked toward the hallway, crossing paths with Malcolm. "What's up? I'm in the middle of something."

"I'm sorry, but I wanted to let you know that after our conversation yesterday, you know, about the drug use in this country, I figured I'd send you a link."

"What kind of link?" he asked.

"It's from *Morning Joe*, an early morning talk show. They featured authors who wrote a book about the opioid epidemic. I thought that from what you told me, it is all the illegal drugs that are causing issues, but this will put some things in perspective. Don't misunderstand me; this isn't going to solve your case, but perhaps the police need to go after all the criminals."

"Okay then," Ramón said, eyes wide open. "I'll take a look at it with Travis. Thanks."

He walked back into the room, and mugshots still crossed the screen with Malcolm looking at them. Travis looked up. "Everything okay?"

"Oh yes," Ramón said. "Maybe we should take a break from this and watch something that aired on a TV talk show this morning about the drug business."

"Probably another story on how we're fighting the wrong war," Malcolm said. "Those talking heads always claim how we should do our job. Presumably, we are fighting the biggest war ever. We just don't have the resources to get us ahead."

"Well, let's see it," Ramón said. "It will give you a break from seeing faces flash by. My head is spinning just from looking from afar." He typed the link into the URL line, and the recorded video started.

The setting was a studio, and there was a split-screen. Mika Brzezinski was on the left; a book's cover was on the right.

Mika: The American Opioid Crisis is worse than ever. With the nation logging a record-breaking 100,000 drug overdose deaths last year alone, most of those deaths were due to Fentanyl, which is fifty times more potent than heroin. A new book out tomorrow, entitled American Cartel: Inside the Battle to Bring Down the Opioid Industry, investigates and exposes how some of the nation's largest corporations created and fueled the opioid crisis. Joining us now are co-authors of that new book, Washington Post Investigative reporter Scott Higham and Sari Horwitz. Good to have you both with us. Sari, I'll start with you. I mean, there was a big case against a drug company pertaining to opioids, but this is still going on, and it seems to be getting far worse."

"It's getting far worse," Sari said. *You know, this is the story in our book about the opioid epidemic that you don't know. Most people, when they think of the opioid epidemic, think of the Sacklers, they think of Purdue Pharma and Oxycontin, but actually, there was a constellation of companies, large corporations in America, some that most people have heard of, household names like Walmart, Walgreens, CVS, Johnson & Johnson, and some that you've never heard of, and we hadn't heard of, uh, one called Mallinckrodt in St. Louis and these companies together basically made and distributed a hundred billion pain pills that they flooded communities all over the country with, and addicted and killed millions of Americans.*

Mika turned to Scott. "Why haven't we heard about these specific cases, and Sari is correct: the Sackler case kind of gave people a sense that this is being dealt with, and yet, it continues? And some major companies that Sari just mentioned are companies that we know very well."

"Well, you know, the Sacklers and Purdue Pharma is an easy target. It's easy to kind of understand if you look at one company and one family, but when you look at the broader picture which Sari and I have done, it took us two years to investigate and write this book. You see that there're so many other companies were far more egregious than Purdue Pharma. Sari mentioned one of them, Mallinckrodt, which is a company we had never heard of. They've been in business for a hundred years. They're based in St. Louis, and they manufactured a blue 30 mg Oxycodone tablet that became so popular on the streets that dealers and users were referring to them and asking for them by name, saying Give me some blues, give me some thirties, give me the M's. This company's conduct became so egregious that the EDA called them a drug kingpin and literally used that term. Mallinckrodt produced 30 times the amount of pills that Purdue Pharma produced. So, there were a lot of companies that were kind of flying under the radar, and I think every time the Sacklers or Purdue gets mentioned, these companies breathe a sigh of relief that they are not being singled out. But, our book calls them to account, and there're many, many chapters and stories and characters who tried to hold these companies to account, and some of them have been held to account, but most of them have not.

Jonathan Lemire jumped in with a question of his own: "Hey Sari, congrats on the book. Some really eye-opening stuff in here. But, walk us through, if you will, what's been done about this? You know the opioid epidemic is out of control in so much of our country, and you paint the portrait here of how that happened *and the web of complicity. What is now the government doing to try to bring this to an end."*

Sari answered: "You know, I wanted to pick up on your point of the web of complicity. This is something we really go into in the book, and I just want to answer that part first. You know, this book is an example of the revolving door of Washington. It really captures how these drug companies lured dozens of employees from the DEA and the Justice Department because they had higher salaries. And, so for higher salaries, they got these employees who were there to protect us from dangerous and addictive narcotics, and they used them to work against the DEA and against the Justice Department. There's an incredible story in our book about how they actually hired somebody from the DEA who helped write a law that undercut, at the height of the opioid epidemic, undercut the DEA's abilities to hold these companies accountable. It is really an amazing story of how Washington works. And so, we tell the story of a DEA agent named Joe Rannazzisi, who had been there for thirty years, sort of a revered agent, and he ran the division of the DEA who policed the companies, who regulated the companies, and he saw what they were doing, and he went after them. He shut down their warehouses, he forced them to pay millions of dollars in fines, and so these companies that Scott and I've just mentioned, they fought back. Especially the drug distributors. They fought back, they took the Justice Department to court, they lost there, so then they went to Congress, and they got a law passed with the help of lobbyists and lawyers that undercut the efforts of the DEA. And then they went after Joe Rannazzisi, and also the Justice Department, at the behest of the opioid industry and Joe was forced out of government. It's a really stunning story of how Washington works."

"It feels like a movie," Mika said. *"And it's a really important story. The book is American Cartel: Inside the Battle to Bring Down the Opioid Industry."*

The program snippet ended, and Ramón closed the browser. Immediately, the last mugshot seen appeared.

"So," Ramón ventured. "That's quite an indictment. Looks like the narcs are partially fighting the wrong war."

"Now, listen, young man," Malcolm said. "There's a big difference between legal and illegal drugs. Our mandate is to stop the illegal ones. The DEA and the Justice Department are to stop the abusive market of the illegal ones. The FDA has to rein in the legal ones. There's still a difference. Don't forget that."

"Oh, I realize that, detective," Ramón said. "This whole Fentanyl business seems to sprout from a demand fed by the legal drugs. I wonder who made the most money, Big Pharma or the illegal knock-offs?"

"Pharma, no doubt, but at least they pay taxes," Travis offered.

"I wouldn't be so sure about that," Ramón said, joining the detective at the screen.

***

After another hourlong session looking at mugshots, Malcolm left, and Travis finished the day's fifth cup of coffee. Ramón rubbed his eyes and drank from his Pepsi can.

"Oh, I almost forgot to tell you," Travis said, leaning back in his chair. "Yesterday, I talked to George Bender. He didn't add anything to the case. Still, he did mention another person in their sleuths group who may be able to tell us a little about opioid use in the Carolina Arbors community. I don't remember exactly what she does, but it has something to do with preventing harm. I think I better call her."

"Interesting, but isn't this something for Malcolm?"

"Perhaps, but I want to hear from her first. After all, I live in that community too."

"Just to be clear," Ramón said. "The Spencers didn't indicate that Fentanyl went to your neighborhood. Most likely, they were sold all over the region

"I understand," Travis said. "I'm going to make that call in a minute. By the way, we're invited to that sleuths meeting on Thursday at 3:00 PM."

"I already know," Ramón said. "It looks like we end up meeting with them every time there's a murder there," Ramón said, taking his drink and heading out.

"Quite fitting, I think," Travis said and opened his notebook.

Chapter 36

Enlightening Travis

Travis pushed the button on a video doorbell at precisely the appointed time. After the familiar dang-ding-dang, he heard a dog barking frantically and a woman's voice shushing it as footsteps approached. The door opened, and the little fluff of black burst out and sat expectantly at his feet.

"Detective Vinder? I'm Barbara Nyles."

He nodded.

"Please come in out of this dreadful heat. Can I get you some lemonade?"

As he entered, she sternly told the dog to come into the house, and it did as she said. It then hopped into its bed and just watched the proceedings.

"Her name is Sprinkles," Barbara started, "I don't know how I would've gotten through this pandemic without her! Anyway, I'm glad you could find time to talk with me during this investigation. I don't know if anything I tell you will help, but I felt it was my duty to talk with you."

Travis walked in as Barbara gestured for him to sit in the yellow leather recliner in the living room. He accepted the offer of lemonade and watched her smoothly bustle around to get two glasses. Efficient, but left every drawer and cabinet open as she whirled through the kitchen. She handed him a drink and sat across from him, placing her glass on a coaster with family pictures inside. As he looked around, he realized that she lived in the same home model he did, yet it didn't feel at all familiar. It always amazed him how there were only twelve floor plans, but each one felt so different once each owner put their stamp on the space.

"Thank you," Travis said, "Your house is lovely. It's the same as mine. I think you have some great ideas on decorating that I may just steal. Anyway, Ms. Nyles, I really appreciate you contacting me. What is it that you wanted to talk about?"

"Call me Barbara, please. I don't have any direct knowledge of anything related to Joe's death," she replied, "I do have some life experience that could be relevant."

"I see. I'm listening."

"Near the end of my career, I dealt a great deal with harm reduction," Barbara paused, "Did you, by chance, catch my lecture for the Community Outreach club?' She continued when he shook his head, "I'm an RN by training, and harm reduction became my thing. I regard it as occupational therapy for people who use drugs. People who use drugs and people who have substance use disorders struggle to conform to abstinence-only treatment modules. Harm reduction recognizes that substance use is a natural part of being human, but what matters is trying to make it as safe as possible rather than prohibiting or punishing it. It also doesn't require abstinence as part of receiving services. A safe supply of substances is a big part of making things safe and reducing harm. Harm reduction as a philosophy can also be found in contexts other than drug use. Some individuals might take the route of Medication for Opioid Use Disorder; we refer to it as MOUD, where they are prescribed methadone or suboxone. Seatbelts and bike helmets are harm reduction tools – they recognize that a given behavior has risk but that the risk doesn't mean we shouldn't do the behavior."

Travis had never heard of harm reduction nor what was involved in trying to help people who have substance use disorders. His *law and order* mentality didn't make room for a tactical approach like this. He tried to keep his expression neutral and opened his mind to listen. He thought he needed to do more of that in all areas of his life.

"Anyway," Barb continued, "Drug use now is nothing like it was when we were youngsters. The addiction statistics are astounding, and they cross all socio-economic boundaries. In reality, the population in The Arbors may be at an increased risk of opioid addiction. The incidents of cancer, joint replacement, broken bones, and other ailments are high, wouldn't you agree?"

"Yes, I never thought I'd participate in conversation after conversation about someone's last doctor visit. Yet here I am. And I've come to an age where sometimes I'm the one telling the story," Travis chuckled.

Barbara smiled. "Over the previous couple of decades, doctors started prescribing Oxycontin and Oxycodone after being assured by pharmaceutical reps that they were not addictive. Also, older people can easily slip into addiction, and sometimes doctors don't consider a person's age when prescribing. Are you familiar with the documentary *Dopesick*?

"Yes, I'm aware of it and the general content."

"I'm worried about dependence on all kinds of opioids in our community. After my lecture, I was approached by several residents. Some were just academically interested. Some had children or grandkids that were or are struggling. A few were struggling themselves, or their spouse was. Still, Carolina Arbors is certainly not exempt from the problem. We need to get people off what they call 'Juice.' I found out most addicted people take it before breakfast...."

She paused a moment and took a breath. "All those conversations were pretty normal, but I had one meeting that struck me as odd."

"Oh, tell me about that," Travis said, taking advantage of Barbara's hesitation after that statement.

"One woman, Joan Spencer, insisted we'd meet away from our neighborhood. On the one hand, her interest seemed to run to academics, but she was highly nervous and emotional. She denied having any problems with drugs herself. Yet, she specifically mentioned Fentanyl, which wasn't something I discussed in my talk. Do you know much about Fentanyl?"

Travis replied, "I know it's a purely synthetic opioid, but much stronger. Unchecked, it can be deadly. I've read that China is a major street supplier, but our doctors also prescribe it. I know there's a drug route going up and down I-95 for all sorts of drugs, including Fentanyl. I don't know much about the distribution or distributors locally, though. I'm in homicide. We have a narcotics unit that works on the illegal distribution of drugs."

Barbara nodded, "All that is true. I don't know if anything I've said helped. It's just that I thought it odd that she would mention it. I also have a favor to ask of you. After this is over, if you're willing, maybe you can help me establish a confidential network to help anyone that wants it. Would that be a conflict for you as an officer? What do you think?"

She drained the last of the lemonade and stood. "I don't want to take up your time. I moved in during the pandemic and don't know many people yet. Would you and your wife like to come to dinner sometime, and we can talk more about my little idea?"

Vinder was pleased with the invitation but a little uncomfortable considering what was happening behind closed doors at home. He said simply: "Maybe after this investigation wraps up. I'll call you, for sure."

Sprinkles came to life as he rose and trotted with them to the door. As he petted her, Barbara casually told him, "Before I forget, maybe you should talk to my friend Charlotte. She knows everyone in this community. Do you know her?"

"You mean Mrs. Beaumont?" Travis said as he reached for the door handle.

"Yes. I talked with her yesterday and hinted she had some important information."

Travis's first reaction was to roll his eyes, but he controlled the urge. "Oh, she's already on my list to contact. Thanks for the reminder, though."

The door closed quietly behind him, and he strolled down the street back to his house, mulling over the idea that people who use drugs were everywhere and he might be close friends with one.

He took out his phone and asked Ramón to call Charlotte. He just couldn't face her right now.

Chapter 37

Enlightening Ramón

As soon as Ramón called, Charlotte hurried to the Durham station. Charlotte admitted that she never wrote down the license place but remembered most of it. She shared all she had experienced and felt regarding Joe Malinski within minutes. Ramón had taken a few notes, and after a half hour, Charlotte left, very content that she'd moved the case forward.

As annoying as Ramón thought the southern lady from Travis' neighborhood seemed, she again had come through. He remembered her well for having wriggled out of a criminal predicament in the first case he'd worked on with Travis. In every other case, as was apparent in this one, she had these little tidbits of information that always seemed to provide a critical clue. The partial identification of the Pennsylvania license plate, the state and the make of the car were valuable. This man clearly had something to do with Joe's murder, but the car didn't match the suspect's. This was a bit of a puzzle, but forensics would clear up the confusion.

His phone rang at his desk. The moment he heard it was Stephan, his heart started to race. "What did you find out?"

"It was an easy one," he heard the familiar voice of the head of the forensics departments on the line. "We got the full tag in no time, and I'm sending you a copy of the registration, the driver's license of a Sam Vanderlaan. We believe the address is no longer a match. That car is mostly seen in this area's cameras, mostly in Raleigh."

"Fantastico!" Ramón exclaimed. "This may be the break we're looking for."

"We've got more than that. We just spotted the Denali on a street cam."

"Where is he?"

"Twenty minutes ago, he pulled in at the Brier Creek shopping area, west of US-70."

"Thanks," Ramón said. He called Travis.

"We got him," he said.

"Who? The killer?"

"Let me look at something," Ramón said, staring at the driver's license on his phone. He continued with slight desperation in his voice. "Not the person we believe to be the killer, but someone who may know him. The picture on the driver's license doesn't look like our suspect. Still, he's of interest if that lady claimed he was staking out Joe's house."

"So, where is he?"

"He's probably having lunch somewhere at Brier Creek. We can be there in fifteen minutes."

"Good luck. I can't go, but have a few squad cars join you. Let them make the arrest and have him brought in here."

"You can count on that, Travis," Ramón smiled.

Chapter 38

Gotcha!

Sam had heaped almost everything on his plate available at the sumptuous buffet at LaBrasa, the fantastic South American restaurant in the Brier Creek Mall. From fish to Asian appetizers to fancy vegetables and fruit and all kinds of bread. You name it, and it was there. *I'll go back later for the desserts,* he thought. He glanced at Carla, the gorgeous girl who had come out from the Erotic Monkey escort service he frequented when he was in Raleigh.

"Looks good, honey?" he asked.

She'd done the same but in smaller portions, like a taste of every item. *She had to keep her trim figure,* he thought. He could almost feel every male in the room looking first at her, then at him with successive lustful and envious glances.

"This is wonderful, honey," she gushed. Her smile filled the room, but he knew it was just for him.

"Come on, dig in."

They began to eat. The food was excellent, and Sam Vanderlaan looked forward to a great afternoon. A new couple bringing packages up from Florida to New York worked out better than he could ever have dreamed. They could make bi-weekly trips, and that more than doubled his commission. He had heaps of money now. Women who wouldn't look at him, let alone go out with him, couldn't keep their hands off a guy with the money he had to throw around. So it wasn't sincere, but who cared? In the end, everyone paid somehow. He spread cream cheese on a half bagel and speared a big piece of lox to finish the little sandwich. A delicious trick he'd learned eating at the delis in New York and Philadelphia.

"So babe, you like that dress I got you the other day?"

"Love it, Sammy. It fits so nicely. Good quality stuff really makes a difference."

They were absorbed in conversation and didn't notice the four undercover policemen entering, one dispersing to each exit door, leaving one who strode over to their table.

"Sam Vanderlaan?" the officer asked softly but with unquestionable authority. "We can do this quietly and without embarrassment for you or the lady, or we can bust your ass and cuff you right here and drag you out the front door."

Sam should've seen them. He looked down while the man talked. It was the wrong shoes. Cops always had bad shoes. Guess that's why they call them flatfoot. Sam knew he was screwed. "Okay, Okay. Let me tell the lady goodbye, and I'll walk out quietly with you. You don't have to drag me out of here. "

It was better they were cops than hoods from up north. He put his hand on the woman's shoulder.

"Carla, honey, I got to go with these men to take care of some business. You finish up your lunch. Here's a hundred. Pay the waiter and take a cab home. I'm sorry I have to leave you alone here, but I promise I'll make it up to you."

"Oh baby, I was looking forward to some fun with you."

"Don't worry, we'll have lots of time for fun," Sam grinned.

Outside, the day was warm and sunny. Most men wore shorts, the usual uniform for retirees in North Carolina. He imagined one of the oglers in the restaurant would be driving her home, to the guy's home, within twenty minutes.

"OK, what did I do?"

"Plenty," one policeman said as he continued reading the Miranda rights."

"Murder?" Sam asked as he was being handcuffed. "Surely, you've got the wrong guy." He laughed as Ramón approached.

"We'll see about that. We're going to ask you some questions at the station. You're coming with us." Ramón nodded to the policeman who had his hand on Sam's arm. The officer pushed Sam into an unmarked car, carefully pushing his head down, and slid beside him. Three cars drove through the congested mall parking lot, then sped up for the short ride to the Durham police station.

In the booking area, Sam was searched, his pockets emptied, and everything signed for and deposited in a yellow manila envelope. He was taken to an interrogation room and left alone for a while. Sam stared at a few blow-up pictures of cardboard boxes in a dumpster. He raised his eyebrows as three men walked in.

"You've already met detective Acosta," Travis said. "I'm detective Vinder, and this is detective Jackson." As he came in, he'd seen Sam stare at the wall with the pictures. "Recognize those?" he asked.

"Looks like some shipping boxes," Sam answered.

"Oh, they were used for shipping, alright," Ramón said.

Jackson showed little patience for a bit of give-and-go, so he took over. "We already know you're working for the Bonelli Insurance company. We also know from a previous case that it's a front for criminal business. So, where do you fit in?"

Sam smiled. "I'm just an insurance agent. I swear, detective."

"With a special interest in what? Covering business in Durham? The ones located in strip malls? The ones you choose to park nearby in the back?"

"What are you talking about? I insure people."

"Have you ever written a policy?"

"I sure have, detective," Sam smiled, shifting uneasily in his chair.

"Be sure to list some of your customers with one of the other detectives here as soon as I'm done with you," Jackson snapped.

Sam didn't answer.

"So, how did you end up in Durham?" Travis asked.

"I moved from Philadelphia a while ago. Older people need insurance too. That's my specialty, you see," Sam answered, seemingly still uncomfortable being handcuffed."

"Stop it already with your insurance bullshit," Jackson said. "We can place you near several places in Durham where illegal drugs were being dropped. We have the pictures. So, tell us a bit about that."

"I go on rides at night 'cause I hate watching TV, so I drive around and observe."

"Observe what exactly?"

"Nothing special."

"You were also seen several times in the Carolina Arbors neighborhood. What were you doing there?"

"I have some customers who have insurance with our company. I visit them."

"And one of those older people you insure are the Spencers, right?"

"I don't have to share my client's information with you, detective. That's confidential."

"And another person living next to them, Joe Malinksi, was another one of your clients?"

"I don't know him. He's not a client, so I'm not sure where you're going with this."

"You'll realize soon enough, Mr. Vanderlaan, that these people are significant in your story. The Spencers happen to be here at the station and have identified you as the person they met in Florida a few years ago."

"They may have bad memories," Sam grinned. "Maybe they take Prevagen and believe that their memory has improved. They're suckers."

"They're willing to testify how you met them in a pizza parlor near The Villages and how you preyed on their need for extra money to offset the medical cost of a family member."

"The insurance premiums are not that high," Sam tried.

"It's not insurance, and you know it, so stop it!" Jackson said, slapping his hand on the table.

"You recruited them to become mules for your drug smuggling activities on behalf of a syndicate. You're not even registered in any state as an insurance agent, so cut the crap and admit it," Travis added, eager to change the conversation to his murder case.

"It's their word against mine," Sam replied calmly.

"Not only theirs," Jackson said, retaking charge. "We have identified one more couple that travels a lot, and we think they spend one out of five days on the road for you. We have you observing the drops and talking with a handler. He's being picked up as we speak."

Sam stared at Ramón, perhaps hoping to get a more favorable comment from the young detective. He met a stone-faced glare.

"I want a lawyer," he said.

"I bet you do," Jackson commented. "You better get more than a lawyer. I suggest two: one that can assist you in the drug case against you and one that can help you with the murder case."

"Hey, wait," Sam said. "I didn't kill anyone, so you know. Murder isn't part of my line of work!"

"But drug smuggling is, right?" Jackson asked.

"I'm not answering any more questions."

"If you're not a murderer, what were you doing outside Joe Malinski's house?" Ramón asked.

"Yes, tell us what you knew about Joe Malinski," Travis said.

"I want to speak with my lawyer," Sam said, ending his first interrogation.

Chapter 39

Linking the Cases

Mrs. Madeline Frazier was speaking on behalf of the Spencers. The couple wore the standard orange DCO overalls, and having been uncuffed after they entered the interrogation room, they were holding hands. Joan hadn't washed up, and running mascara had drawn wriggly lines on her cheeks, one ending at the left corner of her mouth. Fabio looked weary, unshaven, and his hair uncombed. As the lawyer continued, both sat silent, unwittingly mimicking a couple in a scary *Friday The 13th* movie.

"My clients are offering their full cooperation, no matter the consequence, but count on the leniency of the DA and perhaps the court. They've already given you their recruiter, Sam Vanderlaan, whom you already have in custody."

"The DA will be in later, and you may talk with her," detective Malcolm Jackson said. "For now, I need to build a strong case against your recruiter. He's lawyering up, although I haven't heard anything the past hour."

"Perhaps I could have a word with him?"

Malcolm raised his eyebrows and looked at Travis, inviting his opinion.

"I'm not sure he's made a call yet, but I see no problem in it as long as you state that you're representing the Spencers. What are you going to tell him anyway?"

"Some free advice. Is the DA willing to be lenient if he coughs up the big fish?"

"That I can't answer," Malcolm answered. "The guy's kind of a smug SOB. The DA may fry him with the big carps."

"Take me to him," Madeline said.

***

"I didn't ask for you," Sam said after Madeline introduced herself as a lawyer.

"I know, but why turn down some free advice?"

"Okay, shoot. I never turn down a blonde."

Madeline briefly rolled her eyes and sat down. "Listen, Mr. Vanderlaan. I'm representing the Spencers who will testify in court about your involvement in the mules scheme you're apparently running. There's no doubt they'll be considered credible as they are now working with the DA."

"So, you're saying this is a problem for me."

"Not only that, I don't care what lawyer you're getting, but they're going to nail your ass with your attitude and the testimony of my clients and others. I stepped away from their interrogation so that, as I said, I can give you good advice."

"And what would that be?"

"Acknowledge your activities and have your lawyer argue you were taken advantage of in some way. Perhaps you had no choice, or the big guys held something over your head as my clients experienced."

Sam sat back and pondered this option. He stared at the ceiling and then at the boxes. Of course, he knew that the jig was up. For all he knew, they'd produce pictures of him sitting at all those places he shouldn't have been. He had a ton of money in the bank, and perhaps he'd get a short sentence or none. He straightened up. "Okay, I'll get a lawyer who can argue that, but only for the drug case. Tell those guys that I'm not involved in the murder case."

"Good choice. You do realize that the two cases are linked, right?"

"Hey, you're interrogating me now?"

"No, the more info you can provide the detectives, the easier they may go on you. Did you finger the victim?"

"Wait a minute, how do I know this conversation is confidential."

"It is. So, did you?"

"I'd admit that to my own lawyer if I did.."

"Then I suggest you get your lawyer quickly and admit to it. He'll advise you further. I'll not bring up this item because it doesn't belong in the Spencers case. Save your skin as much as possible," Madeline said as she walked to the door.

"Thanks, I'll consider it," Sam said and slumped back in his chair.

Chapter 40

Sam Lawyers Up

Malcolm had stayed with the Spencers and the DA after Travis and Ramón went to the room where Sam was getting impatient. His lawyer had talked to him but had gone outside for another call.

"I hear you've talked to your lawyer," Travis started. "Where is he?"

"He'll be back in a minute," Sam said.

"I hear you want to share some things with us," Travis said.

"I don't mind sharing, but I want to wait for my lawyer. He will want to ensure that my story shows that I'm willing to work with all of you, provided I will get leniency."

"Okay, no problem waiting," Ramón chimed in.

The door opened, and a short and bald man walked in, wearing a cheap suit and reeked of nicotine. Travis noticed stained fingers that held the cigarettes. The man introduced himself as Michael Forrest, Esq.

"Detectives Vinder and Acosta," Travis said. "So, I hear your client is willing to help us in our investigation."

"Which case? I heard there are two," the man asked, blowing his nose in a handkerchief, which he then put in his suit pocket.

"I'm dealing with the murder case, but since it's linked to the drug dealing case, I'll be asking questions regarding both," Travis said.

"My client has expressed interest in cooperating, but only if he's going to be rewarded by the DA and serve no time."

"I'm sure that coming forth will count in the DA's assessment of what charges to file and obviously any outcome in court," Travis said, sitting down. "However, we can't guarantee it."

"I understand your position, but it's just that I want to hear from the DA first before my client tells you anything."

After getting the nod from Travis, Ramón got up and left the room. Travis flipped a few pages in his notebook and flatted them out. He wrote the date, Sam's full name, and the attorney's name on the top of a page.

Durham County DA Amanda Anderson walked in, followed by Ramón. Travis introduced her.

"So," DA Anderson asked, "What are you offering?"

"Wow, you're the max, girl," Sam said. "DA, huh? I'm sure we can do business together and perhaps more."

"Mr. Forrest," Anderson said. "Please direct your client to answer the questions asked of him. His comments or opinions are inappropriate. I suggest you stick to the case."

"And you'll be nice to me if I spill the beans?" Sam blurted out before his lawyer could say anything.

Forrest put his hand on Sam's arm and turned him away from the people at the other side of the desk. The was a brief moment of whispering, and Sam nodded, facing his interrogators.

The DA continued. "Depends. I can't stay, but I want you to sing as loud as you can. You seem to have a flair for the imaginary. Stick to the facts; I want names, dates and places."

"Okay, you got it!" Sam said and turned to Travis. "Where do you want me to start?"

Ramón took the lead. "Why don't you tell us how you got involved with the Bonellis?"

Chapter 41

Sam Sings

Sam told them how he got an offer one day to sell insurance and how that evolved into running important errands. He skipped the part where things were getting too hot for him after a long period of being an informer and cut to setting up drug runs. "Now, mind you, the Bonelli's do not manufacture anything, they are facilitators, and I had to provide the transport from point A to point B. I was assigned to Florida and had to get the stuff to North Carolina and New York. I chose the first because it was more lucrative for me."

"So, who's your contact in New York?"

Sam didn't hesitate. He rattled off the names of his contacts, including Mr. Big, who was running the so-called insurance company in Flat Bush. He even provided telephone numbers and, where known, private addresses. Sam was singing like a true songbird.

"And how did you go about recruiting the Spencers?" Ramón asked.

Sam recounted a friendly meeting in Florida with the Spencers. He turned out to be a good listener as he sat nearby and understood the Spencers' predicament at the time. He continued. "You see, Fabio and Joan Spencer knew it was wrong to play favorites among their grandchildren. Still, little Ellie was something special for both of them, and if they had to pick a favorite, they knew it would be her. They'd been devastated at what happened when she was about nine years old, and *the problem* began. That's what they called it."

"We know their story, Mr. Vanderlaan," Ramón interrupted. "Go on with what you told them."

"I could do that, but to understand that, I need to tell you what I heard and how I became their savior, you see."

"Alright, go ahead," Ramón said.

Sam dove back into his story. "They cared for their Ellie, who had always been artistic—drawing little pictures when she was three—getting better as she grew older. Grandpas and dads got artistic crafts projects on holidays and birthdays. Who couldn't resist a giant orange ladybug made of paper mache on father's day? Better than any tie. It had been great for the Spencers until *the problem*."

Travis looked at Ramón, who took a deep breath, waiting for the part where he recruited the couple.

Sam didn't seem to have noticed as he continued in great detail. "Ellie's artwork improved until some time after her seventh birthday. The drawings began to be less natural. Lines became wobbly. No one could tell what her pictures represented anymore. *The problem* was scientifically known as Metachromatic Leukodystrophy or MLD for short. I looked it up."

"And what's the disease?" Travis asked.

Sam smiled as if he was flattered by someone asking for his knowledge. "It's a rare genetic disorder that damages the fatty sheath around the spinal cord and nerve cells. It affects every part of a child's life. Feeling and tactile sensations like touch, pain, heat and cold disappear. Then motor skills like speech, swallowing, vision and hearing are degrading. Memory and thinking fared no better. Vision and hearing were next."

It sounded to the detectives as if Sam was reading a monotonous medical book. He took a sip from the cup of water in front of him. Then he continued and proved to be quite the expert on the treatment.

"I didn't need to research the disease or the treatment because the Spencers volunteered it all, you see. They told me that Ellie's parents earned a nice living, but not nearly enough for the avalanche of medical bills they ran up. Insurance was a joke. It's an orphan disease, so rare that insurers didn't even have billing codes for treatment or costs. After insurance, out-of-pocket was projected to be close to half a million. It might as well have been a million dollars for Ellie's cash-strapped parents."

The detectives figured out how Sam preyed on the couple. Travis wanted to back up a little. "So, tell me more about meeting the Spencers?"

"I overheard them discussing the situation at an NYPD Pizza in the Villages. I needed people like that, and my glib spiel about how I could help retirees earn a lot of extra money hit a cord. Given that they were anxious to share their grief with anyone who would listen, they turned out to be perfect as I had been trolling for new drivers."

"So how did you convince them to become mules," Ramón asked.

"I maintained a concerned expression on my face while listening. Still, inwardly, I was elated to find the couple desperate for extra cash and probably willing to do anything to help care for their ailing granddaughter. I pitched without telling them what they were to take up north."

Travis interrupted. "So, what did you tell them," he asked.

"I told them I had associates who needed packages privately transported from Florida to North Carolina. It's valuable stuff, and they like to keep it confidential. They tried UPS and FedEx, but deliveries were often late, and they were afraid of packages sometimes getting lost. When Fabio asked the obvious question, I told him it was nothing illegal. These were personal items that would be best moved by private parties. We'd pay them 10K for each trip."

"Obviously, they weren't suspicious of the goods they were to smuggle," Ramón said.

"Right, they were overwhelmed by Ellie's illness and the expenses their son was facing for the expensive drugs Ellie needed. They were in no mood to ask what was in the packages or anything else. They quickly agreed to give it a try. The 10K per trip seemed like a lot of money for the relatively short drive. Still, they told themselves it was for Ellie and were lucky to have come across the opportunity."

Ramón was annoyed with the story, especially since it made Sam seem to be a good guy, compassionate and understanding, providing an innocent solution to a financial problem. Ramón was equally pissed about missing out on a quiet lunch with Lydia at La Mez restaurant on Page Road. He wanted to get back to the murder case and get this guy behind bars, but not until he gave up the organization and the killer. "So, it's obvious that you saw Mr. Malinski as a threat to your operation here. Who did you contact to remove that obstacle?"

Sam thought about Joe's butting in where he shouldn't have. Clearly, that started a sequence of events that landed him in a room with pale green walls. He wondered if every damn police station and jail in the country bought their pukey-colored green paint from the same place. He realized he was stalling, but he had to appear magnanimous in giving up the killer and Mr. Big so he would never see another room like this again. He knew the fewer lies he told, the easier it would be to keep them straight when they repeatedly asked him the same questions. Sam was glad he had a tight alibi when the retired snoop cop, Malinski, bought it. They never give up on cop killers, though. That was for damn sure. He'd give them a few other mules since they seemed to know about them anyway. But not now. Only when he'd do this all over again with Detective Jackson. He needed to focus and saw that the detectives were getting impatient. "So, I told you I tracked him to his house."

"What did you do next?" Ramón asked.

"I told my contact in New York."

"Mr. Big?"

"No, one of his lieutenants."

"Name?" Travis asked.

"Billy Mason. He deals with problems on the fringes."

"Is he the killer?" Ramón asked.

"No, he's the guy who hires the heavies, you know."

"Do you know any of those characters?"

"Never met one. I'm not in the killing business as I told you."

"Do you have any names?"

"I don't."

"How did you communicate with Billy, and what did he tell you?"

"I called and told him that we might have a problem. I gave him Joe's address. Billy told me he'd send someone."

"When was that?"

"Months ago."

"When did you hear that something was to go down?"

"At the end of June. I told them that the ex-detective was sitting on whatever he had discovered. The Spencers were out of the picture, address unknown, so there was no urgency. But I held Malinski responsible for that. Something had to be done."

"So, you got Billy involved again?"

"I lost important mules, and even though I was lucky to find super mules, they cost me a chunk of my cut. And yes, I called Billy. I think he sent out a guy at the beginning of this month. Once the guy was in place, it was out of my hands. I don't want to deal with issues like that."

"So, you set up Joe Malinski, right?" Travis asked.

"Yes, I admit to that. I was never told he'd be killed. Billy also hires enforcers, you know, people who can make people talk."

"Really? You just told us that he was a fringe problem that needed to be dealt with. What do you think that meant?"

Sam leaned back, putting clasped hands behind his head and waited briefly to answer. He sighed and then responded. "It did cross my mind that he'd be dealt with harshly. Listen, I gave you Billy's name. You can find him at the Flatbush office."

"Oh, we certainly will," Ramón said. "I want you to look at this picture and identify this person of interest." He pulled out a photo from the Arbors video, enhanced by the forensics, showing a reasonably good image of the suspected murderer.

Sam held the sheet with both hands and studied the face for a few seconds. He put the copy down. "I've seen him, but I can't give you his name."

"Where have you seen him?"

"In Philadelphia, years ago."

"Care to explain?"

"It was at the time I acted as enforcer, and he was involved in a shake-down situation in a case I worked on."

"You worked over the same client, but you don't know his name? C'mon, that's hard to believe," Travis said. "Think a little harder."

"I really can't recall. Maybe it was Matt or Pat perhaps. I'm not sure."

"Okay, that's something," Travis said as he nodded to Ramón. The latter took Sam's phone out of a bag and handed it to Sam. Travis continued. "Why don't you give Billy a call and ask him if he's sent Matt or Pat down yet?"

"Why? He knows that Malinski's gone. He'd assume I know that, so why would I ask him about it?"

"Tell him you're good with removing the threat and thank Matt or Pat for the job."

Sam unlocked his phone and hesitated. "What if he knows I've been taken in?"

"You've been here less than two hours. How would he know? Just put the call on speakerphone. Keep the conversation light and brief. Make sure to tell Billy everything is fine on your end."

"Okay," Sam said and made the call.

The detectives listened in, and Ramón recorded the short conversation. The killer's first name was Patrick.

Chapter 42

Who's Patrick?

Ramón felt pretty good about how the interrogation with Sam went. He doubted that the DA would really come down easily on Sam Vanderlaan. Travis was on the phone with his counterparts in Philadelphia and New York. They'd also help Malcolm, but more importantly, it might shed more light on the killer who was more critical to their investigation. They left Sam with Detective Jackson to divulge the details on mules and the transportation of drugs. Travis was sure that only the complete capture of the network from Florida to New York with all the bad players would be regarded as favorable by the DA. He was glad this wasn't part of his job.

Back at his desk, Ramón called Lydia. "How's your day going?"

"Great! I'm really looking forward to this weekend. It's hard to believe we've known each other for one year. I'm glad we're celebrating this. Can you tell me yet where we're going?"

"It's a surprise until we're on the road," Ramón smiled. "It will be fun, guaranteed."

"I just don't know what clothes to take."

"Summer clothes and a bathing suit."

"Are you talking about a swimming pool or a lake?"

"Now, now," Ramón said. "Fishing for where we're going again."

"We're going fishing on a lake?" Lydia laughed.

"No, silly."

"How long of a drive is it?"

"Less than two hours."

"So, we're staying in North Carolina. The beach?"

"Yes and no, but that's enough questions. By the way, you do realize that we may have an issue if something develops in our case. For now, Travis is taking the lead, so even if we don't get the killer by this Friday, he should be able to handle it. There's a small chance I might have to go to Philadelphia, but I hope not."

"I, too, hope not. That would ruin our fun," Lydia said.

"I agree. Anyway, I'm picking you up around 5:30 PM."

"So we should get there when?" Lydia tried.

"In time for a great dinner," Ramón laughed. "You're killing me. See you then, bye."

He hung up and smiled, looking at a flyer for a bed and breakfast place in Little Washington, known as the best romantic getaway place in the state.

***

When Ramón walked to Travis' office, the call with Philadelphia ended. "How did it go?" he asked.

"It went well," Travis said matter-of-factly. "I just sent a picture of this Pat, uh, Patrick to the department there. We should hear something soon, I hope."

"Did you call your contacts in New York? What was it? Queens?"

"I did that first. Once I told them what was happening at Bonelli's Insurance office, the DEA agents would be all over that place. I thought that business was gone after we'd gotten the boss, but now that there's a Mr. Big, who knows what they're involved in? My primary objective is identifying the killer and finding out where he is."

"Assuming they can identify this guy, he's most likely out of state, so there's not much for us to do."

"I agree, but I still want to follow up regularly. The guys in New York were especially pissed that one of their own was killed. Believe me; this will have top priority."

"I get it. That's good. Listen, aren't we supposed to go to that Sleuth's club tomorrow afternoon?"

"Oh crap. I'd already forgotten. There's not much we can do there, but I know George and Charlotte are counting on it."

"I heard that Mary's a member as well. This may be a little too sensitive for her. Perhaps George should give her a heads up that we'll discuss Joe's case. Can't be easy on her."

"You're right. I'll give him a call. In the end, it's her decision, of course."

"Right," Ramón said. "I'm heading back to my desk to write a report. Oh, and how are you doing?"

"Well, it's still a mystery of what's going on with Maureen, man. I've gotten my own place for about a month, just to give her space. I'm going to see her tonight to have another conversation. I'm hopeful."

"I get it. Also, I'd like to get out of here Friday mid-afternoon. I'm taking Lydia to a B&B for the weekend."

"You guys are serious, aren't you?"

"Well, we've known each other for a year and want to spend some time away from our usual hang-outs, job, family. You understand."

"Good for you, Ramón. Hope you have fun, you two."

"Oh, Lydia's great, and we'll have a great time."

"Enough already. I see you're practically drooling over her. Get out of here."

Ramón laughed. "Okay, call me as soon as you hear from either Philly or New York."

Chapter 43

Jail Time

Attorney Madeline had good news and bad news for the Spencers. She decided to start with the latest on Ellie. The last treatment had gone well, and she was on the mend and expected to recover and ultimately be disease-free. The couple hugged each other and cried.

"Your son would like to visit you tomorrow. How do you feel about that?" Madeline asked.

Joan shook her head.

"We don't think we can face him in this condition," Fabio said. "I'd rather hear from the DA first. Have you heard?"

"That's the other news I have," the lawyer said and paused.

The Spencers could tell that all was not well with that part of their predicament. They squeezed each other's hands tightly, appearing on edge. "What did she say?" Fabio asked, his voice quivering.

"Well, she's determined to keep the charges as they are. The case is being turned over to the United States Department of Justice, as is the norm with drug smuggling. It's up to the DA in that office to review the current charges. You'll likely have to appear before a United State District Court Judge. I'll meet with that DA and stress that you both have no priors and were not apprehended in possession of any illegal substance. Furthermore, you have been very forthcoming in your statements. While all these things are positive, there're different rules in the federal court system. A judge will most likely enforce the law and impose a prescribed penalty. That would mean a federal prison sentence."

"That's terrible," Fabio said while his wife started to cry silently. "What can we expect?"

"I'm afraid it's up to the judge, but I venture to say it would be two years. Also, there's no parole in the federal system."

"Will we be able to appeal?" Fabio asked, putting his arm around a sobbing Joan.

"Most likely. I must tell you that it will be expensive. The good thing is that you may not incur any financial penalties, except for court costs, given that you spent your gains for a good cause. Still, the court does not regard a Robin Hood-inspired crime as anything different from a regular crime." Madeline paused.

"If it's a federal prison, where would we be?"

"I'd ask the judge for a minimal correction facility like Butner in our state."

It remained quiet for several minutes. Nobody moved, but the sobbing continued. Fabio was curious.

"What's going to happen to Sam? And have they caught the guys we dropped off the packages with?"

"Mr. Vanderlaan will spend quite a bit more time in jail. I don't expect too much leniency. And yes, all the handlers have been picked up, and they'll appear in court soon. Believe me; you two will receive the lightest possible sentence."

"But that's two years of our few remaining years," Joan said. "I realize we did wrong, but we'd miss so much of Ellie's growing years now that she's going to be okay again."

"Rest assured; I'll argue all that with the judge when the case is in court. I will go for probation, but my chances of going against the guidelines are small. I just wanted you to know that. The judge could impose a recommended six-year sentence in the worst case, although I don't think it will come to that."

Fabio sighed. "I reckon that's the price we're paying for helping out our granddaughter. We can be proud of the fact that we could give the money. If we don't have to give it to the state or the government, that would already be a win. I think we should look at it that way and hope for probation."

"That's the right attitude, Mr. Spencer," Madeline agreed.

"What about the other case, the one about our neighbor Joe who was killed?"

"You're not named in that one, but everyone in your community will know that your actions indirectly caused his murder."

"So, we'd have to move?" Joan asked.

Madeline nodded but didn't answer. She was sure the Spencers would figure things out as time went on, whether in jail or not. They'd need much support from their son, and Ellie would always be a bright star in their sky. She was sure they'd get that and learn to live with the consequences of their actions. She also hoped there would be no further links to them through the smuggled drugs. There'd been several overdose cases in the past year, but it would be hard to prove the Fentanyl came from the packages smuggled by the Spencers. That would be another permanent blight on their lives. Not knowing would be as hard as the guilt of being responsible for a person overdosing. Hopefully, when the case details became public in their community, it would discourage others from becoming mules.

Chapter 44

Luring the Killer

Before Travis got to his desk later that afternoon, the headquarters in Queens and Philadelphia both identified the killer. The detective was given the name of Patrick Conelly, wanted for murder in each city, but his address or whereabouts were unknown. At least it was a step forward, and good to know that he and Ramón weren't the only ones looking for him. The problem was that it seemed entirely out of their hands, now that he had most likely gone back to where he came from. Adding one more murder to his list might not improve the chances of Conelly being found by his colleagues up north.

Ramón had already suggested coming up with a ruse to lure the killer back, but Travis couldn't see that happening. Yet, there must be a way to expose Conelly so he could be arrested. It was a job for the police forces in the cities that already had him on their radar. After throwing some ideas back and forth, Travis did have an idea. "What if we make it known that the Durham Police were close to identifying someone as the murderer of Joe

Malinski? Not that we'd use Conelly's name. We could get the word out, saying someone had taken a picture of him and his car. However, that person was afraid to share it with the police for fear of retribution."

"What would that do?" Ramón wondered. "It would just make him feel safe. What's more important, how would we get that message to him? It's not that we can send him an email or use any people at Bonelli's to let him know. I don't think that would work."

"We could make it appear like that person was about to go to the police with the information."

"Again, how would you let him know?"

"Let me think about that," Travis answered. He recalled having been in this situation before, but this was still different. He rubbed his chin while staring at the ceiling.

"Can we get his cell number?"

"That Billy character probably has it," Travis said pensively. "Then what? It's not that we'd call him."

"No, not us. I was thinking of Mary."

"What? Mary? Why would she do that?"

"Look at it from the perspective of Conelly," Ramón answered. "We know he was scouting Joe, kept an eye on him at the bocce ball courts and most likely on their walks. He must have seen Mary with Joe several times. If he remembers her, he'll know that she's credible."

"Right, and he'd want to prevent her from sharing whatever she has on him with the police."

"And putting her directly in harm's way if he should act on it," Travis said. "Perhaps not a good idea after all."

"We could prevent her from getting harmed," Ramón suggested. First, we could see if he bites. When he does, we set up our teams in her and Joe's house. It would be like him running into our arms. Mary would be out of sight so that nothing would happen to her. What do you think?"

Travis nodded. "It could work, but it would have to happen fast. We can't have a guy like this taking too much time on this. He either shows by tomorrow, or her deal is off. Let me run it by the captain and the DA. Meanwhile, why don't you call this number at the precinct in New York and tell them Billy needs to share the killer's cell phone number with us."

"I'll do that right now," Ramón said as he took a paper handed to him.

"Good," Travis said. "If we get the okay, we need to speak with Mary soon.

Ramón walked back to his desk and placed the call. He briefly explained what they planned to do and was told twice that it wouldn't work. He insisted on getting Conelly's number from the man in their custody at the Queens' police station. He pleaded with them to call him back ASAP. Before he got an answer, Travis walked up. "We've got one shot at this," he said. "And only if Mary agrees. She's mentally vulnerable now, and we'd be adding a physical threat. We can't force her."

"I fully understand that," Ramón said. "I talked to the detectives in Queens, and I'm waiting for the call. Why don't we check to see if Mary's home and pay her a visit."

Travis returned to his office to make that call while Ramón remained at his desk, staring at the phone as if he were willing to ring. A half hour went by as Travis returned. "Mary's a hundred percent in," he said. "She is willing to send the guy a text. We'll figure out what she should write when we visit her later. Any word on the phone number yet?"

"No, but they have my cell. Why don't we head out to the Arbors?"

"Sounds like a plan. I need to go there anyway. Better to give Maureen a heads up for tonight," Travis sighed heavily.

Twenty minutes later, they pulled up in front of Travis' home. He walked in the front door when Ramón got the call.

"Did you get a number?"

"Billy came through," the New York detective said. "We had to make some promises, but it worked. Now let's see if your little plan works. I doubt it will, but hey, you never know how a blind man catches a hare."

Ramón frowned at the strange expression but then wrote down the number in his phone's note section. Travis reappeared, red-faced, and slammed the door shut. "Off to Mary's house," he snapped and loosened his tie.

***

Mary welcomed them at the door. The dark circles around her eyes betrayed her continued grieving at the loss of Joe. Travis would do all the talking, and seeing her like this calmed him. He'd tread carefully.

"So basically, we have a good picture of the murderer. Ramón will put it on your phone. All you need to do is send a message to him with the image. We hope that he panics and high-tails it to North Carolina. He already knows where you live, and we'll be here with you, ensuring you're safe. We'll arrest him the moment he enters the neighborhood, your street, or comes near your house. We'll also have a team on standby at Joe's house. Are you okay with all that?"

Mary nodded. "What do I send to him?"

"Give me your phone," Ramón said. He air-dropped the enhanced picture to her phone and entered Conelly's name and number in her contact list. He then got everything ready to send the message, which he also typed in. He handed the phone back to Mary. "Read it and click on the send icon when you're okay with it. Then, we'll wait."

Mary read the message after staring for a moment at the picture of the man that killed her friend. She took a deep breath after reading the text one more time: **Hi. I tracked you down. I know you killed Joe. I have seen you. I will send this picture to the Durham police tomorrow at 5 PM. I am a single woman, and 25K would make me erase the picture. I will not negotiate. Do not come here. Contact me, and I will tell you how to pay me.** Mary nodded and pressed the send icon. "It's sent," she said calmly and put the phone on the table. "I guess now we wait?"

"Yes. He'll respond soon enough," Travis assured her. "He will agree but not really pay. He will want to silence you. It may take him a day to get here."

"Wait a minute," Mary objected. "What if he's still in North Carolina or Virginia?"

"We have counted on the fact that he may be closer than we think. The entire team will be here at your house and in Joe's in the next fifteen minutes. As I told you over the phone, we are taking you to the Marriott nearby until this is over. We'll stay with you there, check his reply, and help you lure him here tonight. After we leave, two policemen will be outside your door."

"Okay," Mary said. "I hope I did the right thing. Are we leaving now?"

"As soon as the teams are dropped off," Ramón answered.

"Perhaps you'd like a cup of coffee?" Mary offered. "It makes it easier to wait."

"Sure," Travis said, smiling for the first time today. He and Ramón sat back, staring at the phone on the table while

Mary walked over to the kitchen area in the large living space. Soon, the smell of freshly brewing coffee was wafting through the room.

Mary returned with cups and stopped to stare at her phone for a second. She waited for the brewing to complete and then poured the coffee. "I guess he isn't in a hurry," she said.

"He may not read your message for quite a while," Travis explained the delay.

"What if he calls?"

"Don't answer, but tell him to text you only because you don't want people to overhear your conversation."

"What if he asks me where I am?"

"Tell him you're at an event at the neighborhood center."

"Okay," Mary said and took a small sip of the hot beverage. "By the way, you haven't told me where you got the picture of the murderer."

"He was spotted in the parking lot at the clubhouse and the outside cameras. Our forensics team was able to blow it up and enhance it."

"Did you know him?"

"No, we didn't," Ramón responded. "He's wanted in New York and Pennsylvania, and they recognized him."

"I see," Mary said and rested her hands on her lap.

It remained quiet for a long while until there was a knock on the door. Mary jumped up and ran for a bedroom.

"No need to panic, Miss Valero," Ramón assured her. "It's one of our guys."

Travis had walked over to the door and opened it. He had a short conversation with three men and had them wait outside. He turned to Mary. "They're going to set up in your garage. You have windows in the door, and they can keep an eye on the front of your house without being seen. Another team is placed in the back area where they can keep an eye on the back of your home. The third group is going to be in Joe's house."

"Okay. Can I get those men anything," Mary suggested.

"No, they're all set. Thanks," Travis said. "I suggest we leave now. Do you have your travel bag ready?"

"Yes. Do you want me to leave any lights on?"

"A small one would be fine but close your blinds. The guys will open them up in the morning."

"All right then," Mary said. "I guess we're ready to go." She picked up her phone and turned off a few lights.

The detectives walked her toward Travis' car. Mary stopped and looked back at her house with weary eyes, seemingly uncomfortable. As she took off with Travis, she sat in front, and Ramón followed to the hotel in his own car.

Chapter 45

Setting a Trap

Mary settled into the hotel room. Travis and Ramón were determined not to leave until the killer had made contact with her. Not wanting to talk about the case, Mary steered the conversation toward things happening in the neighborhood. Ramón was already aware of the parking in the driveway issue. It was still good for a few laughs. When Mary told them about the architecture nazi, a title she'd dreamed up about a person who roamed all the streets, looking for small to large infractions of the rules set by the architecture committee at Carolina Arbors. She didn't necessarily object to the need for people to stick with the principal regulations. However, she thought that counting solar lights in yards was ridiculous. *Who does this*? she had asked. It's not normal. She was convinced that the lighting situation around the clubhouse violated those same rules.

"I live here, and I'm unaware of these rules," Travis said. "Then again, I don't subscribe to the CA messages. I just don't have the time for it."

"I think it's funny," Ramón said.

"You should get room service," Travis said, looking at the time. "It's been over two hours, and he hasn't reacted yet. I also need to call my wife." He walked out to make a call in the hallway.

"Can I choose anything?" Mary asked.

"Whatever you want," Ramón said. "Not sure how good the restaurant is, but that's your best bet for food tonight." He waited until Mary had made her choice of salmon on pasta. He called in the order for her.

Travis was still outside when Mary's phone rang. She leaned over. "It's him!"

"Let it ring," Ramón said, putting his arm on hers.

Travis walked in when Mary's phone pinged, letting her know a voicemail was waiting.

"Aha, he called?" Travis asked.

"Yes," Mary said. "Let's listen." She turned on the speaker as they heard the voice of Patrick Conelly.

"Hey, Mary, I guess. I got your message. Look, it sounds like a lot of crap. Don't know what you're talking about. I don't know how you found me, but it sounds like someone set you up. So, do whatever you want with the picture. Call me back if you dare."

The message ended, and Travis nodded. "Not unlike what I expected: doubting you have the goods on him and alluding that perhaps you had help from the police. His last comment is an attempt to scare you off. Typical."

"So what do I do?"

"Mary, we stick to what we discussed. You'll send a text back. Ramón, why don't you take a stab at it?"

Ramón took the phone and started typing: **I'm an excellent sleuth. I know you scouted our area. Don't call me. I won't share my conversation with others. 5 PM is the deadline.**

Travis approved, and Mary sent the message.

"He'll get back to you soon now," Ramón said.

The answer came immediately: **You drive a hard bargain. Are you home tomorrow? I can send money around 4 PM – Let me know your bank account info for a wire.**

Travis smiled. "He's buying time to get here. Tell him you'll send the bank info in the morning. Also, tell him you'll be home all day."

This time Mary typed the message herself and sent it. "What do I do now?"

"Have dinner and try to relax this evening. I'll be back in the morning. Remember, there are two men outside your door. They'll rotate out later tonight and in the morning. Don't leave your room and you'll be fine. At any rate, don't leave the hotel until either one of us tells you it's safe to do so."

"Thanks, detectives," Mary said. "I hope he comes to our neighborhood and you guys can capture him. I'll feel a lot more relieved."

"I understand," Travis said, and Ramón nodded as a way to say goodbye.

When the detectives had left, Mary slumped in on a couch and had a good cry. Dinner would be a diversion.

Chapter 46

The Sighting

As promised, Travis showed up at the Marriott at eight in the morning. He was curious to hear from Mary, mainly to see if the killer for hire had contacted her again. Although there was little analysis available on Patrick Conelly, Travis had a hunch that the guy didn't like loose ends. If he was correct in his assessment, Conelly would show up to deal with Mary. He was convinced the murderer would never pay the money she'd requested. He expected Conelly planning to be at the Arbors very briefly and was counting on the fact that Mary would be home. Travis figured all the men in place would act in a coordinated way and arrest the man before he got to Mary's house.

The dinner tray from the previous night was still on the hallway floor. Two policemen were standing by the door to Mary's room. He said hello to the men and knocked on the door. Mary removed the security chain and let him in, smiling briefly. "Thanks for coming," Mary said. "I was going a little crazy here."

"Oh? Good morning, Mary. What's up? How were your evening and night?"

"Not so good. Couldn't fall asleep at first, and when I finally did, I woke up several times imagining someone was trying to get into my room. I know it's silly because there're men outside. I ordered breakfast, and I saw them when they brought it in. I felt a little better at that moment. Oh, and I already got a text from that guy."

"What did he say?"

"He said he has the money in cash and would drop it off shortly after lunch."

"Did you respond?"

"I didn't yet. I wanted to mention it to you first."

"In that case, just send him a thumb-up emoji. No need to elaborate."

Mary did precisely that. "Done," she said. "What do we do now?"

"Well, first of all, my hunch was right. This criminal is coming after you, and he will walk right into our trap. We plan to follow him when he drives into the neighborhood and close in on him before he can get to your street. We'll arrest him away from all the homes. We're also ready for him near your house on the off-chance that he'd make it there."

"I can't wait for this day to be over," Mary said as she held her cup of coffee tight with both hands. "I'll be glad when you have captured that man," she said and paused, staring out of the window at a wooded area. An Aqua water tower was ruining an almost perfect nature scape. "I realized this man must have seen Joe and me several times. He knows what I look like, and that scares me, you know."

"Well, he won't get close to you, I promise. We'll lock him up, and he'll probably serve years in jail here and then up north. He'll never get out. I wouldn't worry about him," Travis assured her.

"If you say so," Mary said. She put all the dishes back on a tray. "Oh, I'm sorry, did you want a cup of coffee? There's plenty here, and I think there're some cups here."

"I've had some already," Travis said. "Listen, I've got to go, but stay in touch; you've got my number."

"I do, detective," Mary said. "Do you think he'll contact me again?"

"Perhaps. He may text you as he gets closer to ensure you're indeed at home."

"What if I can't reach you?"

"You've also got detective Acosta's number, don't you?"

"I do."

"And if he doesn't answer, tell one of the men outside to get in touch with us via radio."

"Oh, that sounds good. How will I know that it's safe for me to leave here? Will you call me?"

"I will, but just in case, the men outside will be informed as well. They may tell you before I have a chance to call you."

"Good. I haven't taken care of my email for the last three days. I'll spend some time on my laptop while I wait."

"That will keep your mind off things going on. But please don't worry. You'll be fine." Travis got up and walked out. He briefly talked with the men outside and headed for the Arbors.

Back in his car, he called Ramón. "Everything okay where you are?"

"Yes, sir," Ramón replied. "All entrances to the neighborhood are covered. We'll get immediate feedback when his car is spotted on cameras on US-70, the Leesville fire stations and along T.W. Alexander Drive. That's if he drives the same car, of course."

"Have you heard anything from the Virginia people? They're checking on I-95 and US15."

"Nothing from them, but their calls will be delayed for sure. Too many cars to check."

"I get that, but that would be ideal for us to calculate when he could get to the neighborhood."

"Copy that. I'll call you when we have a sighting."

"Be prepared to check out every driver coming into the neighborhood in case he has switched cars. Everyone has a picture of him, right?"

"All taken care of. Traffic has calmed a bit, and it's getting easier."

"Good. I'm heading home briefly, then the station, and I'll see you at the clubhouse by lunchtime."

***

Ramón and two officers staffed the small command center at Piedmont Hall. Everyone on the stake-out had been delivered lunch, and the rather dull operation continued. The Virginia State Police hadn't called in, and regular contact with the men at the various locations around the neighborhood produced negative reports. Ramón was getting anxious as they expected Conelly to arrive between now and 4:00 PM. The plan was for the team who spotted him to follow his car to the designated spot off Del Webb Arbors Drive on the dirt road under the power lines, heading west. A construction roadblock was ready to deploy at a moment's notice. The equipment was in place. Neighbors might experience a short inconvenience as they'd be redirected away from the scene so that the killer would be the only one taking the dirt road. An assault team was set up around the first bend on the dirt road. Others would follow his car, and the trap would shut.

Ramón reflected on the slight complexity of the plan, especially the part where they had to make sure that Conelly would be the only one on that dirt road. Travis walked in and interrupted his thoughts.

"Everything okay here?" Travis enquired.

"All set. We should hear something soon."

"I hope he drove that BMW. We were smart not to have included that in the picture."

"Fingers crossed, I say," Ramón replied. "How did it go at home, I mean last night?"

"Nothing much to add. I just picked up some fresh clothes. We're still not where we need to be. I'll be spending some more nights away."

"Sorry to hear that, Travis," Ramón said.

"Thanks. Anyway, can you check with the Virginia police? They should have spotted him by now if he's getting here soon."

"On it," Ramón said and tapped in the digits. He listed for a few seconds after he told the person on the other end why he called. He shook his head and said *Thank you* as the call ended. "We have to be patient," he said to Travis.

"I know. I just wish we could be better prepared as to the time. That's all."

Ramón nodded and pondered the problem of steering the suspect off the road. He'd get suspicious. What if he turns around and drove toward another access point? When he'd see the same equipment from the other side, he'd know it was meant for him. He'd high-tail it out of the neighborhood, that's for sure. Then what?

"What are you thinking, Ramón?" Travis asked, seeing the concerned look on the young detective's face.

"I think he may be smart enough to recognize a trap. I think we should stop him on Del Webb."

"In a way, I agree with you, but he will be armed, and you know what can happen. We must get him far away from houses for the neighbors' safety."

"Are the guys ready for when he tries to evade the trap?"

"Yes. That's when it will take place on the main street. He will be surrounded by cars and will have no way out. In that case, I'm hoping he won't even contemplate shooting. I don't think he's ready to die in a gun battle."

"Let's hope it doesn't come to that, even on the dirt road."

"Amen," Travis said.

It had been quiet for a while until reports came in. No sighting was reported until the call from Virginia. Ramón was excited. "Did the cameras spot him?" The answer was affirmative, and after jotting down some info, he hung up. "We're in luck. He's in the same white BMW, spotted twice. Once outside Richmond at 11:30 AM and again at 11:50 at the exit of I-95 to I85!"

Travis smiled. "That's great work. That should place him, barring any stops, at the Arbors around 2:00 PM. Alert everyone that he's been spotted and give them the ETA."

Although still nervous, Ramón appeared happier. He shared the news on the radio. Everyone was now on alert.

***

Mary was startled by the knock on the door. She looked through the spy hole and was relieved to see one of the officers. She opened the door.

"We've got him, Ma'am," the officer said.

"Really? Where?"

"I heard that he'd been spotted. That can only mean one thing: they're about to get him in custody."

"Whew, now that's good news. I guess you're off duty now, and I can get home."

"I still need confirmation from the detective, Ma'am," the officer responded.

"I understand. It shouldn't take that long," Mary said. "Let me know when I can get out."

The officer resumed his position outside, and Mary closed the door. Back at her laptop, she finished sending an email.

At least an hour had passed since the officer had told Mary about possibly having the killer in custody. But why hadn't either of the detectives called her? It couldn't take that long to apprehend that Conelly guy, could it? She called Travis' number and got his voicemail. She had better luck with Ramón. "It's me, Mary," she said. "One of your guys outside told me the man was spotted over an hour ago. Do you have him in custody, detective?"

"He was spotted on I-95, not here. Perhaps it'll be an hour or so until we spot him here. Then it will go quickly. Just sit tight, and we'll let you know, Miss Valero," Ramón said.

"Okay," Mary said and ended the call.

She returned to sit at the small table, eating a few left-over chips from her lunch. She looked at her phone after she heard an alert. *Crap,* she thought, *I have the book club meeting at three.* She was responsible for the book report on Delia

Owen's *Where the Crawdads Sing*. She had to lead the discussion but heard that the detectives might join the Sleuths. If that were the case, they'd discuss the murder of her friend Joe. That's something she wasn't ready for. Given the circumstances of apprehending the killer this afternoon, that discussion may very well be pushed to the meeting in September. That would be a relief. The best thing that could happen is that nabbing the murderer took place before 3:00 PM, freeing her up and keeping the detectives busy in Durham.

Mary looked over the notes she had made for the book report. She wanted to stress that the story is powerful, rich and sad. She would mention that the author had past experience with murder and mystery when working in Zambia; however, the book wasn't based on a true story. After reading her report, she turned on the TV. She could use some distraction, and it was easier to wait for the call that would bring so much relief. Just thinking of Joe made her eyes water. She blew her nose and watched a re-run of *The Carbonaro Effect*. She felt all the unsuspecting people were quite gullible. Often she was able to figure out how the tricks were done. People on the show didn't reflect on what they witnessed as magic and acted totally flabbergasted. She, too, smiled for the first time today.

Exactly at 2:00 PM, there was another knock on the door. The officer she'd talked to earlier was back. "Sorry about the misunderstanding before," he started. "This time, the message was more precise. The man we're after has entered the neighborhood, and the latest chatter indicated he had fallen for the trap they set."

"Finally," Mary said. "Let me call the detective, hold on."

Mary called Ramón, who answered immediately. "Did you get him?"

"Hey Mary, I'm going where he will be cornered soon. It's a matter of minutes until we can take him into custody."

"That's good and timely as well. I really wanted to go to the book club meeting this afternoon."

"That shouldn't be a problem. One of the officers can take you home then."

"At last," she said and turned off her phone. She turned to the officer stills standing in the doorway. "You can take me home. Let me gather my belongings, and we're out of here."

The officer nodded. Mary stuffed lingering items in the small overnight bag, glanced over the room from end to end and indicated that she was all set.

Chapter 47

The Squeeze

The stakeout group near the top Leesville Road entrance had no problem recognizing Conelly's car. His face was recognized quickly as he slowed down to turn into the neighborhood. The huge Caterpillar excavator was positioned across Del Webb Arbors Drive, allowing cars to turn only left or right onto the dirt service road. Flagmen were to direct all vehicles to the left and only steer the white BMW to the right.

Ramón had joined Travis about two hundred yards from the turning point onto the dirt road. A well-armed assault team was ready. They took their positions as soon as the signal came in that Conelly had made the turn as directed. Meanwhile, police cars stationed out of sight on both sections of Currituck Lane rushed onto the main thoroughfare toward the service road. The squeeze began.

Conelly was tired and in no mood to argue with the flagman about the detour he had to take. That didn't mean he wasn't pissed about it. He had no idea where the service road ended. Still, he was familiar with the neighborhood and felt comfortable finding Mary's house.

He touched the gun in the holster under his left arm. He wanted this to be a quick job. He'd have enough time to attach the silencer on his walk from the car to her house. He checked the brown manilla envelope on the passenger seat. He grinned: *a cheap rolled-up newspaper pretending to be 25K.*

He slowed down after the first couple of heavy bumps. With his foot still on the brake pedal, he swore when he saw two police cars with flashing lights in his rearview mirror. He had no choice but to speed up. He screamed, mad about the cops, as he turned around the curve. His gut clenched when he saw a black armored vehicle in front of him. There was a slew of police cars and at least twenty heavily armed men pointing their assault rifles at his car. Quick thinking was needed.

On both sides of the service road, he noticed wooded areas. The trees on the right were a no-go, but he estimated the heavy brush on the left could be overrun with his BMW. He headed straight for the bushes, crashing into the unknown. He didn't care about his car. He needed to get away fast. Suddenly his car went downhill and stopped nose down in a small creek. He pushed open the driver's door and ran up the hill on the other side of the stream, shielded by the bushes. Houses! That's all he saw. *Perfect,* he thought and ran toward the back of a home on Bloomsbury.

The assault team or the police officers following Conelly's car had seen that coming. He disappeared in a flash into the wooded area. Travis was shouting for the men to give chase. The problem was, they couldn't see him. Ramón was with the men, and they soon ran up to the ditched white car. The suspect was gone. The team spread out while Travis commanded the patrol cars from the street to return and cut the killer off on the next road. A non-cooperating Caterpillar excavator slowed this down. They, too, abandoned their vehicles and ran toward the next road on the right while shouting and holding their guns ready.

Patrick Conelly knew he was in a pickle, but so far, so good. He heard all the yelling behind him, and it sounded like he had a good lead on the chasers. He ran between two houses and crossed Bloomsbury, briefly looking left and right. No cops! He kept to his left until he reached a section stretching between two rows of houses. There were plenty of trees that he ran through in a zig-zag fashion. He hadn't heard any more shouting for a while and stopped briefly to look back. Not a soul in sight. He kept running through the back yards until he hit a big street. He immediately recognized where he was: the clubhouse was sitting to his right across the road.

Travis knew that Conelly was running. He was mad about their failure to squeeze Conelly's car. Damn! He told the men to spread out to the back of the houses and make their way down along the streets and back yards. He had already called the teams stationed off Palmer Hill and Andrews Chapel Road to hurry to the clubhouse. From there, they needed to move up toward Bloomsbury. One by one, the police cars loudly arrived in the parking lot. Armed officers ran and spread out.

Conelly was about to run across the road when he heard the sirens nearing the street. He suddenly remembered that this was a 55+ community, and his best option to blend in was to stroll. He walked to his right and made his way to the second entrance to the parking lot. At that time, the police cars kept piling into the parking lot, and a quick look to his left confirmed what he had hoped. They crossed the road and headed for the area he had just come through. No one paid any attention to him. He crossed the lot to the enclosed garbage area and crouched behind the container. He knew this wasn't the best place, but he would move once all the cops were out of sight. He realized he was in a quandary. Since the police are involved, would he be able to get to Mary's house? Perhaps it was better to get out of the neighborhood altogether. As he stood up because his legs started to cramp, he deliberated the options again. Should he high-tail it out of the area or stay to complete the job? She was a witness, and now all of Durham's finest knew about him. His rage got the better of his thoughts, and he clenched his jaw as he thought about Mary. *The bitch set me up!* Yes, he would finish the job! He could quickly get to her place using the walkway behind the clubhouse. But first, he had to make sure the cops didn't cut off his path.

The two search groups met up somewhere between Bloomsbury and Carolina Arbors Drive. Emptyhanded. Travis was pissed. "Did anyone coming from the clubhouse see a younger man running?" No one had. Travis had to think quickly. He contacted the men still at Mary's and Joe's house. He informed them that the killer was loose in the neighborhood. One of the men spoke up. "Detective, I just wanted you to know that Mary came back already. We were surprised because we knew that the perp was somewhere nearby. We tried to stop her, but she had an urgent meeting. She drove off minutes later."

" Hang on! "What the hell? Who dropped her off? She knew not to leave where she was until I gave the go-ahead!" he yelled. Hold on. Stay on the phone!"

Travis turned toward Ramón, who had walked over, hearing all the shouting. "Did you tell Mary she could go home?"

"Of course not," Ramón said, wide-eyed. "Why would I do that?"

"Did you talk to her?"

"Yes, she called, and again the officer told her that Conelly had been seen. This time in the neighborhood."

"What did she say to you?"

"She had a meeting at three in the clubhouse. I told her it may not be a problem, but I would let her know."

"Dammit! She didn't hear it that way. She figured we'd have him by now! I can't believe this!"

He swore and called everyone together. "The assault team will head for the clubhouse. The rest of you keep checking this area. Knock on every door. We can't let this killer get away with this."

As the group dispersed, he resumed his call. "Listen. I want you to be on alert. I have a feeling the killer will still want to get to Mary. He'll worry about how to get away from here after that. Call me when you spot him!"

Travis didn't wait for a reply. He joined the group that was already heading for the clubhouse.

Chapter 48

Taken

Mary pulled into the parking lot. She was early, but that's exactly what she wanted. She got out of the car, carrying a large purse with her laptop. She halted when her phone rang and experienced a pang of anxiety when she saw it was detective Vinder. "Hello," she said.

"Mary, what are you doing out of the hotel?" Travis yelled. "Where are you anyway?"

She took a deep breath and answered in a calm voice. "I understood from my conversation with detective Acosta that the arrest was imminent. What's going on?"

Travis lowered his voice, yet the situation was dire. "Mary, listen. We didn't get him. He's running free in the neighborhood. Where are you?"

"I'm in the parking lot at the clubhouse."

"Good, stay there. I'll be there in a minute. I'm coming with the swat team that you should see momentarily. Are you closer to your car or the clubhouse?"

"My car."

"Get back in it and hide. Please, Mary, you could be in a compromising situation."

Mary panicked again. *When was this going to end?* She opened the car door and got in. That's when she dropped her phone.

Patrick Conelly couldn't believe his luck. Looking out for the cops, he had briefly left his safe spot to peer at the goings on in the parking lot. There was Mary, standing by her car, phone in hand and totally oblivious to what was about to happen to her. He swiftly moved between the cars, making sure to stay out of her line of vision. He was a car away when she opened her car door. He saw part of her face. She seemed upset. Was she being warned? He couldn't let her get in the car and take off. He had to act quickly. He ran from behind her car as she got in and dropped her phone. He slammed her upper body into the passenger seat, quickly moved her legs over and jumped in. He snatched the keys out of her hand and started the car. It had taken all of five seconds. It didn't bother him that Mary was screaming bloody murder. He drove off, taking a left out of the parking lot.

Travis was searching that area, trying to remember Mary's car. When he spotted what looked like her car, he was alerted when he saw it drive off. She had said she would stay. Then he got it. It was a man driving the vehicle. The killer! He motioned Ramón over. "Your car is here, right?"

"Yes."

"Get it. We need to follow that car!" He observed Conelly take another left.

"Why?"

"Hurry, I'll explain in the car."

Ramón sprinted for his car and picked up Travis on the road. Travis called all cars and at least one sniper back on the *road* to head for the area between Bloomsbury and Daniels Post Court. He knew they could cut off the killer as he had only one way to go: the lower end of Bloomsbury.

At the direction of Travis, Ramón took a right on Daniels Post and drove as fast as he could. Their car came to a screeching halt in the middle of Bloomsbury, blocking the road and not allowing a right turn.

Conelly sped up a bit, but he had no choice but to put on the breaks. He slammed the steering wheel. *I should have driven faster*, he thought, but it was too late now. When he considered a quick U-turn, cars with blaring sirens and flashing lights commanded the street behind him.

Travis figured they finally had a squeeze with no escape possible this time. Except for the one problem, of course. The hired killer had a hostage, Mary. He stared at the car in front of him. He'd been in these situations before. It never had a good outcome for the suspect. The victim often didn't make it either. Being driven into a corner, the subject would think in a panic and do irrational things. It also made him vulnerable. He had a feeling that, somehow, this case may be a little different. A seasoned killer with a hostage. Travis realized he had to protect Mary at all costs. A few minutes passed in what now appeared as a stalemate, allowing the entire swat team to show up.

Conelly, too realized what was happening. He was facing a multitude of assault rifles again. He slowly pulled his gun out of its holster. No need for a silencer this time. He told Mary to sit up straight. She was petrified but somewhat relieved, seeing that they were surrounded by cars and people. "Give yourself up," she said. "Look out there."

"The hell I will. You'll see; they'll let me go," he snarled back. He put the gun to her head. "Don't move, or I'll pull the trigger."

Mary froze, and she saw that Travis had taken a step back. Travis realized he had to start talking to the killer. Anything to keep him from killing Mary. He put his gun down on the road and raised his hands. Moving closer to the car, he started talking. "Let her go. Don't hurt her, and we won't hurt you."

Patrick had only one message: "Let us go, or I'll shoot her."

Travis shook his head. "That's not going to happen, and you know it!"

Mary easily heard the conversation through the open window. She'd seen many movies with scenes like this. She moved her eyes left to right without moving her head as the barrel seemed glued to her left temple. She was hoping to see a sniper, a guy who could take the killer out with just one shot. But what if the gun still went off? She stopped thinking about that scenario. Perhaps talking with him could prevent all the shooting? "Hey, it's okay if you don't want to give me the money," she said.

"Oh, you're funny, lady," Conelly said. "I wasn't going to give you anything."

"I figured as much," Mary said. "Listen, why don't you give yourself up? I know the detective, and he likely has a sniper somewhere. Maybe he's aiming at you now...."

"You watch too much TV, bitch. Sit back! I'm going to drive over the curb and past that detective's car. We'll be out of here in no time. Sit tight and hope the trigger doesn't go off with the bump."

"But you still would kill me, so what difference does it make to me if you get out of here or not?"

"Think you're smart, huh? You're the one who got me in this mess. I should've known it was all a ruse. Damn woman. Oh, there is Mr. Detective again."

Travis had walked up to Mary's car again, no longer with his hands in the air. "You know, Conelly, there's no way out of here. So put down the gun and get out of the car."

"You watch!" Conelly barked and put the car in drive with his left hand. He turned the wheels toward the curb. He inched forward just a bit, making sure about the lineup. It would be bumpy, but he'd briefly use both hands.

Mary noticed that with a little nudge to the wheel, the car would actually run into another vehicle parked on the street. She, too, realized that he couldn't do what he wanted without using both hands. She made up her mind.

"Don't move the car," Travis commanded.

Conelly yelled back, "Hasta la vista," and floored the pedal. Before they hit the curb, he quickly put his right hand on the wheel. Just what Mary had hoped for. She lurched to her left, grabbed the wheel and jerked it toward herself as hard as possible. Two seconds later, her car slammed into a parked car.

It all happened so fast. Patrick Conelly was thrown forward, his head hit the steering wheel, and the gun fell on the dashboard. Mary didn't wait. She felt a surge of pain but managed to open the door to the car and run toward the front door of a house. Travis approached the crashed car. Conelly was clearly dazed but aware that he had to get his weapon. By the time he reached it, Travis had his service gun at the head of the killer. "Easy boy," he said. Two policemen ran to the car, one entering on the passenger side. Moments later, Conelly was handcuffed and dragged out of the vehicle.

Meanwhile, Ramón had dashed over to Mary, sitting with her knees pulled up to her chest and arms wrapped around her legs. "Are you hurt?"

"My shoulder's killing me, but it's better than the alternative.

"That's for sure!" Travis said. "Let's get you checked out at the WakeMed Emergency."

Chapter 49

One Month Later

Upon entering the conference room, all the sleuths stood and applauded long after Mary sat down. Mary raised her hands and nodded to everyone around the table. She opened her laptop and waited for the club president to start the meeting. Before George could say anything, Travis stepped into the room.

"Hi, everyone. I wanted to stop by and thank you for all your help. As usual, we owe members of your club for the contributions that were very helpful in our investigation. You made us aware of drug mules, odd behavior in the neighborhood, the extra dangers of illegal Fentanyl, witnessing suspects and most of all, you helped us catch the killer. Mary, that was a daring move that day. The applause was well deserved. However, I hope you'll never have to go through something like that again."

The fellow sleuths applauded again and thanked Travis for stopping by. Travis reassured the group that he would make himself available if they needed anyone to talk to.

George started the meeting and reminded the members that last month, they had decided to push Mary's book report to the next meeting.

Mary opened her laptop and stared at the screensaver: a picture of her and Joe at a restaurant months ago. Before she clicked on her report file, she briefly sat back and reflected: *Regardless of what happened that day, the case had been about the man she'd started caring for, the man who made her smile again, with whom she enjoyed dinner and long walks. It was about a life cut short and lives together upended. All their plans were squashed; there would be no more walks together, no more going out, no traveling to faraway places, no cuddling on the couch to watch a silly movie, and no more sweet lovemaking.* She knew grief was about love and loss; at that moment, she longed even more for Joe.

She took a deep breath and sat straight, briefly putting her hands flat on the table next to her laptop. She clicked on the icon and started: "Now, does anyone know what the word *crawdads* means?"

THE END

Made in the USA
Columbia, SC
18 September 2022

67457667R00146